THE TIKI KING

THE TIKI KING

Stories

Stacy Tintocalis

◆

Swallow Press
ATHENS, OHIO

Swallow Press / Ohio University Press, Athens, Ohio 45701
www.ohioswallow.com

To obtain permission to quote, reprint, or otherwise reproduce or
distribute material from Swallow Press / Ohio University Press
publications, please contact our rights and permissions department at
(740) 593-1154 or (740) 593-4536 (fax).

Printed in the United States of America
Swallow Press / Ohio University Press books
are printed on acid-free paper ⊗ ™

18 17 16 15 14 13 12 11 10   5 4 3 2 1

"The Tiki King," "Another Kind of Sleep," "Iron," "The Last Perfect Day,"
"Pirates," "Bill Suggs' Safe House," "Honeymoon in Beirut," "Too Bad
about Howie," "The Man from Istanbul," and "Geishas" first appeared in
the following journals respectively: *Crazyhorse* no. 75 (2009); *Fiction* 19, no.
1 (2004); *Cream City Review* 31, no. 1 (2007); *North Atlantic Review* no. 15
(2003/2004); *Event* 34, no. 1 (2005); *Santa Clara Review* 96, no. 2 (2009); *Post
Road* no. 18 (2010); *The Journal* 33, no. 2 (2009); *Packingtown Review* no. 2
(2010); and *The Atlantic* (Fiction for Kindle).

Library of Congress Cataloging-in-Publication Data
Tintocalis, Stacy.
  The tiki king : stories / Stacy Tintocalis.
     p. cm.
  ISBN 978-0-8040-1126-6 (acid-free paper) — ISBN 978-0-8040-1127-3
(pbk. : acid-free paper) — ISBN 978-0-8040-4042-6 (electronic)
  I. Title.
  PS3620.I563T55 2010
  813'.6—dc22

2010010132

Contents

TOO BAD ABOUT HOWIE

No Beatles. No Beach Boys. Not even a little "Me and Bobby McGee." Too cheap for music, that's what Wal-Mart was. You had to shop to the noise in your head. Gone was the Rodgers and Hammerstein era when my mother wore curlers in the market and my old man smoked Pall Malls in front of the beer coolers. Nowadays nothing but crying babies and single mothers filled Wal-Mart. Nobody noticed the chumps like me who foraged for red-and-white tins of McCormick nutmeg.

So I was on one of my Saturday night shopping sprees, carting by Campbell's Cream of Mushroom, Campbell's Tomato, and there she was—Sally—my ex-wife. I only saw a snapshot of her in the aisle's open aperture before—poof!—she was gone.

When I reached the Wonder Bread aisle, I caught another glimpse of Sally. There she stood, the woman I'd almost spent my life with, and she was practically a stranger to me.

I watched her squeeze a loaf of wheat bread and had the strong urge to pinch her waxy cheek between my thumb and index finger to see if she, too, was still fresh. Before I knew it, she carted away, so I abandoned my cart by a Wheat Thins display to follow her.

Two years of marriage. That's how long it had taken to navigate the peaks and valleys of my ex-wife's personality. Little did I know that her emotional topography included unmapped islands littered with human skulls and enormous Easter Island statues staring out at the sea. She was one hell of a mystery island: quiet on the outside but cannibal-infested within.

I caught up with Sally in the cold air of the dairy section, where she was opening a pink carton of eggs to check that none were cracked. Her hair was pulled back in a professorial bun that revealed her pale neck. She hunched over her shopping cart like the Grim Reaper, wearing the same black cardigan she'd always worn around the house.

"Hopper," she said. "I know you're behind me. I recognized the sound of your walk." Without turning to face me, she put her eggs beside a six-pack of Swiss Miss chocolate pudding and some Lean Cuisine frozen meals. Back at the Wheat Thins display, my own cart must have looked pitiful with its tin of nutmeg, case of Coors, and bag of Iams hairball care cat food.

When Sally turned, it was the first time I'd seen her in months, and I winced at the sight of her face. Her apricot-toned skin looked coarse, and her eyes were veinier than they'd been just ten months earlier, when she'd packed up her stuff and left.

"Your new hair color looks good," I said, shuffling like a schoolboy. A stray auburn hair clung to the shoulder of her cardigan. I resisted the urge to pick it off.

"You like it?" Her eyes brightened, and it almost sounded like the old days before she sicced those cannibals on me. "It covers all the white hairs from the divorce," she said.

"Ah, Sal, don't be like that."

"What do you expect?"

I shrugged. "So, how's Howie?"

"Itchy," she said. "Fleas."

"Well, Morton still craps outside the litter box." I waited for her to say something. "Lately he's been on a puking spree," I continued, "leaving me little puddles of vomit all over the hardwood floors."

She shook her head in a perfunctory way, as if it didn't really matter to her that Morton was puking a lot. Just twelve months ago, we would have spent a whole dinner conversation on the subject. "And what exactly did the puke look like?" she would have asked, her little heart breaking.

After two years of marriage, our pets were our only significant joint property. She got Howie, the Weimaraner, who was hers to begin with. I got Morton, the cat.

And who was taking Howie for walks up to Shooting Star Bluff, I wanted to ask. No doubt, the divorce had caused Howie to succumb to licking his crotch excessively. "Too bad about Howie." That's what one of Sally's colleagues from the French department said when he ran into me at 9th Street Video, knowing how tight Howie and I had been, how we used to walk Columbia's trails and romp around town together.

"You know," Sally said to me, her eyes direct, "you don't have to talk to me every time you run into me, Hopper. We can act like we never met. We can be strangers."

I exhaled through my nostrils and said, "Fine," even though nothing about her was strange, nothing in her voice was unfamiliar, not even her body was unknown to me.

I walked back to my cart, thinking I'd write about our encounter in a book Sally once called my *Book of Bad Ideas*. I'd write about the arc of Sally's neck before she'd turned and the way her back stiffened like a wall between us, and I'd write something about the fierce urge to bite her scalp as hard as I could. Then I'd finally write:

> *The back of your ex-wife's neck*
> *is a stranger's blank face.*

Before I moved to Columbia, Missouri, I was a low-rent actor in Kansas City and Branson and St. Louis. Musical theater mostly. I sang, I danced, I did a little soft shoe. Seven years ago I was doing *The Fantastics* at a dinner theater, getting paid smack wages that didn't cover the cost of gas, when I finally got a decent gig doing matinees of *Mary Poppins* each weekend for a heavily funded kiddy theater in downtown St. Louis, the kind with a kids' art gallery full of finger paintings and a hands-on art experience where toddlers can squish their fingers into clay and draw sunshiny pictures of their parents. Kids would come into the theater smelling of Play-Doh and bubblegum. Midway through the performance they'd start bawling and asking, "Where's Daddy?" while I danced and sang my heart out playing the part of Dick Van Dyke. So I "Chim chimineyed" away each weekend until the show's three-month run and my meager finances finally ran out.

After that, I followed my girlfriend Mary to Columbia and got a gig teaching composition. Columbia's one of these land-grant college towns planned around state parks and an old railroad converted into a bike trail. A regular hiking boots and gourmet coffee kind of place. In a matter of weeks, Mary dumped me. Then she traipsed around town with an art history grad student named Ludwig. From then on it seemed like Columbia was strategically planned for awkward run-ins with ex-lovers. I'd see Mary and Ludwig at cafés, on campus, at the health food store. I didn't get over Mary until I was introduced to Sally, a newly hired French professor who didn't know anyone in town.

Now don't get me wrong, I was still unsure of Sally at the end of our first date. While I sat in her dining room waiting for coffee to brew, her dog Howie roved around my legs under the table. The warmth of his body pressed my inner thigh. Then his brown nose came snorting up between my legs after nuzzling my crotch.

Dinner had been the usual rigmarole of bad takeout Thai food and life histories: Me, I went to the University of Kansas. Majored in theater. Minored in creative writing. Got an MFA in poetry just for kicks. My old man would have flipped. A tough guy like him, someone who'd worked in an auto salvage yard, he would have looked me in the eye and said, "So you're one of those damn fairies I see on TV, is that it?" Luckily my mother understood my desire to perform and saw me in *The Music Man, Oklahoma,* and *Jesus Christ Superstar* before her death. She's the one who taught me to sing. She had albums of all the musicals by Rodgers and Hammerstein and Irving Berlin, and in harmonious times, she'd pull out *South Pacific,* and we'd stand in the kitchen drying dishes and singing "Bali Ha'i." My father hated it. He'd be sitting in the living room watching *All in the Family* yelling for my mother and me to "Shut the goddamn up!" as he so delicately put it.

Sally's life history was more to the point:

1. Graduated with honors from the University of Chicago.

2. Went straight to a PhD program at Yale.

3. Got a job.

"What about boyfriends?" I asked as Sally poured us cups of coffee.

"What about them?"

"Weren't there any?"

She shrugged. "I dated a guy named Mark for a year."

"No drug overdoses? No suicide attempts? No stints in mental hospitals?"

She shrugged again. "I'm pretty normal."

To tell the truth, it was the dog that made me stick it out that first night with Sally. We'd moved to the living room couch, and Howie put his mouse-brown chin on my lap.

Then he looked up until I finally scratched his head. Afterward he put his paw on my thigh and snuffled me with his nose, asking to be smelled back, and so I did: I put my face against the dog's velvety ears and inhaled his musty scent. In return, Howie rolled onto his back, paws pedaling the air, and gave me that come-hither dog look with his mouth hanging open and his pupils big and black, begging for a little cootchie-coo.

Goddamn if Howie didn't talk to me that night with all his meaningful looks and gentle nudges. It made me want to forget about Sally and get naked with the dog. I wanted to wrestle him to the ground and straddle him.

And Sally, poor Sally, how I pitied her and the way she dressed in frumpy sweaters and uptight turtlenecks, nothing revealing her tiny waist or her apricot-toned skin. So unlike the needy actresses I used to date who smoked clove cigarettes and drank whiskey straight from the bottle. By my mid-thirties, I'd had dozens of short-term relationships with women who slept all day and worked all night at bars or casinos. None of them were like Sally: straitlaced, stable, well employed.

Later that night, after the coffee and conversation had run dry, Sally seemed lonely and withdrawn when she called to her cat Jojo across the house, saying, "She's a sweet kitty once you get to know her."

Sally was still too shy to make eye contact. Her little turtlehead barely poked up from her cable-knit sweater. Howie sat beside Sally and mooned his eyes at her. There was something tragically romantic about the two of them—the way Howie gazed at her with unapologetic affection, the way Sally gazed back with nothing but love.

"Howie usually doesn't like strangers," Sally said.

"Dogs get me," I replied. "They always have."

"Howie gets me, too." Then Sally smiled for the first time all night, and it gave me this twinkling inside my chest that made me think, hey, this woman's all right. I could even live like this. A cozy home. A sane woman. A loving dog. It might be nice.

When I left, I stood in the doorway and clasped Sally's hands, lacing our fingers together like a strange fleshy flower. Then I gave the meat of her palm a gentle love bite. "Goodnight, Sally," I said, "Farewell, Sally," except I sang it to the tune of "Goodnight Ladies," and it all must have been very appropriate because she kept smiling at me as I walked away singing, "We're going to leave you now." There we were, totally incompatible, a 21st century Marian Paroo and Harold Hill from *The Music Man;* Sally was no different from the uptight librarian played by Shirley Jones, and I was nothing more than an emotional opportunist who knew right then and there what kind of man I had to be to make Sally fall in love with me. And, no, I wasn't that kind of man at all. Too moody. Too restless. I tended to wake up in the middle of night and walk the fenceless backyards of Columbia where I'd see people watching TV inside their homes and wonder what it felt like to cuddle under a crocheted afghan and just stay in one place for the rest of my life. So no, I wasn't the kind of guy to settle down with a French professor. But it occurred to me I was also an actor: I could play the part. If I felt like it, what did it matter? In the world of musical comedies, everyone is mismatched. The professor marries the street urchin. The Salvation Army officer marries the gambler. The librarian marries the traveling con man. In the end, everybody gets what they want, and not what they really deserve.

Six months after running into Sally at Wal-Mart, I had the summer off and made a new lady friend, a redheaded legal secretary named Teresa. The night I met her, I was at a bar wearing one of those blue mechanic's shirts with a white oval patch that said "Ike" in navy embroidery. I'd found it at a thrift store and couldn't resist. Most people called me by my last name—Hopper—but I liked the idea of being called Ike for a change. Something about that Ike shirt lifted me out of a long blue funk I'd been in since the divorce. It got me singing that old presidential campaign song for Dwight D. Eisenhower:

> *I Like Ike.*
> *And Ike is easy to like.*

"Yo, Ike," Teresa said. "This round's on me."

A bartender filled our shot glasses with whiskey. Then we went for round two. The next thing I knew, I was waking up in Teresa's bed, and she was humming a song to herself as she made breakfast. While Teresa fried some bacon and eggs, I put on my Ike shirt and stepped onto her deck to gaze down a grassy slope at all that Saturday morning sunshine. Wind chimes played on the breeze. The air smelled of fresh-cut lawns and new beginnings.

Teresa's deck overlooked a large mowed lot where one neighbor's yard blended into the next. Nearby were the decks of two other homes. And what do you know! There was my old friend Howie curled up in front of his redwood doghouse, no more than one deck away.

During the divorce, just before we'd left our old house, Sally mentioned she was moving to a subdivision with unfenced backyards that receded into woodsy evergreen groves with property lines demarcated only by the height of the grass. "A home that's good for Howie," she'd said. I'd never seen the place.

From Teresa's deck, I let out a long two-fingered whistle, and Howie's head perked up from its sleeping position, his ears at full attention. Suddenly I felt like little Roddy McDowall in the classic film *Lassie Come Home.*

"Howie," I said. Even though it had been sixteen months since I'd last seen him, Howie stood up on all fours, alert, ears pricked. He had that "come get me" stance with his front legs pushed out: if I'd made a sudden move, he'd have charged straight into me.

Later that week, I did a little online spying and found out Sally's schedule of summer-school courses. Turned out she was *Qu'est-ce que c'est*-ing her way through an Intensive French course that lasted four hours a day, from 10:00 a.m. to 2:00 p.m., five days a week. So after Teresa smooched me good-bye in the mornings, I'd watch *The Today Show* for a few hours, then go down the slope to visit Howie.

The first time I went, I paused outside Sally's bedroom window, listening. Inside was our old bed, the same sunflower bedspread we'd used, the same wicker bookcase, the same oval loom rug. Everything was the same except it wasn't *ours* anymore, and it had all been picked up and put down somewhere else. Nothing had really changed for Sally, I thought. She'd probably imagined going to the Humane Society and picking out a new husband the way she'd picked out Howie, a place with caged men in suits sharing pens with mutts like me. And I was the kind of wild-eyed mongrel they'd put to sleep after two weeks, the kind no one really wants to bring home.

On Sally's back deck, a bag of potting soil sat beside some geraniums and an unfinished cedar window box. Sally's bird feeder was empty, though a few chickadees still flew across the yard from a tall pine tree to peck at the seedy remains. Seeing all those singing birds and our old life reminded me of the beginning of our relationship when we were like characters from *The Music Man* and everything seemed so harmonious. I was always singing, and Sally was always smiling. When I was in a loving mood, I'd sing

"Getting to Know You" from *The King and I*. And when I was feeling perfectly in character—perfectly Harold Hill—I'd sing "Marian . . . Madam Librarian" to my little Shirley Jones.

Howie had been sleeping in his doghouse, delinquent in his guard dog duties. When I turned from the bedroom, there he was, wagging his tail so hard that his whole body shook. He looked good but heavier in the gut, no doubt from not being walked enough. Even his facial fur looked paler, his jowls more hangdog and loose. His mouse-brown fur appeared ashy and older. Howie was chained up, so we just sat on the steps of the deck and reminisced about old times—run-ins with unleashed dogs in the park, swims in the creek, and long sprints into the woods whenever I biked the MKT Trail.

The following Monday, while Sally was teaching four hours of French, I unchained Howie and took him out to Grassland Trail. I'd missed the way Howie would run ahead of me and snuffle around looking for field mice or rabbits. Howie once dove his nose into the snow and brought out a fat brown mama mole, and all the brown babies came squirming up with their panicked pink snouts searching for her. Howie was a bad dog that day. He ran off with his trophy mole in his mouth. Meanwhile Sally yelled after him to "Put back the mole!" But Howie didn't come back right away, and Sally started crying for the baby moles in the snow, each of them a bent brown thumb against a bed of white. When Howie finally returned, the mama was dead, and I took the mole and buried it with the babies back underground where they belonged.

Toward the end of our marriage, walking Howie was the only thing Sally and I did together. I'd reverted back to my true self. Irritable. Restless. Sleeping all day, writing all night. Sometimes I'd take a nip of whiskey when Sally was sleeping, or I'd run off with the dog to get away from her. So it was on one of those final walks when I was singing "Seventy-six dog bones" to Howie that Sally asked, "How is it that you have all this time for the dog but no time for me?" From the look on her face, I could tell the island drums in her head were beating; the cannibals were sharpening their spears.

"You can't throw tantrums and run off with the dog and expect me to roll over and forgive you when you come home."

We'd been walking Howie on a street behind our house. Sally folded her arms like she was cold and tightened her black cardigan around herself.

"I think we need to split up," she said.

"I'm not ready."

"Well, I was ready six months ago," Sally replied.

"But I had no idea anything was wrong."

"Well, something *has* been wrong," she said, "and it's been wrong for a long time. Haven't you noticed how depressed I've been? You sleep all day, for Christ's sake. Couldn't you figure out you were neglecting me? Couldn't you tell I was sick and tired of the bullshit antics with the dog? And all that manic writing in your stupid book! Well, I've read your book," she said quite firmly. "You keep asking why I haven't finished reading it. Well, I finished it a long time ago, and it's nothing but a book of bad ideas," she said. "I've been trying so hard to keep my mouth shut, but I can't keep it shut any longer."

When we got back to the house, Sally was crying. None of the cats were around. Not our newly adopted cat Morton. And not Jojo, who'd begun pissing so much that we had to put her in our rumpus room downstairs. It was after midnight when Sally came out of her office and went to the basement litter box, only to find Jojo on the bathroom floor shaking.

During my third week of summer dognapping, I tried the sliding glass door to Sally's house and *Bingo!* Must have been my lucky day. Sally wouldn't be home for another three hours, so there I was in her dining room where she'd left a baggie of dog biscuits on the table. Thoughts started cycling through my head about what to do first, where to go, which thing I should steal. I couldn't leave without committing an act of emotional vandalism.

There was this particular spatula that Sally had made off with, and I'd been missing it so damn much ever since. It was a little beige plastic number with the words Log Cabin on the handle. Perfect for flipping flapjacks without scratching the bottom of the pan. One day I'd chased Sally around the house with it, smacking her on her bum like a little girl, and she giggled and shooed me away, saying, "Stop it, you jackass! Stop it." Anyway, this particular spatula had sentimental value, so I went into her kitchen, which she'd prissed up with some ceramic containers for flour and rice, and started pulling open drawers. By God, there it was, next to the bamboo tongs and soup ladle. Funny how when you see something you haven't seen in a long time, your brain does a little somersault, and that's what my brain did, not expecting to see those old tongs. My brain went "TONGS! Holy shit! Tongs!" And then I threw open all the cabinets and loaded up on spices that I'd purchased. Sally wouldn't be using anything like allspice or cardamom or the queen of all spices, saffron.

There'd been a mango chutney I used to make that Sally raved about, and I'd been the star of academic parties for months. "Did you bring the chutney?" people would ask the minute I walked in the door. "Yes, yes. Of course I brought the chutney." My fifteen minutes of fame fizzled out when the wife of a Spanish professor came up with a new-fangled guacamole. Anyway, for a moment I imagined what it would be like if I made Sally mango chutney right now, with Sally finding me naked in her "Look Who's Cookin'!" apron. How could I be threatening in a getup like that? She'd have to laugh, wouldn't she? She'd have to say, "Ha ha. You asshole. You made me chutney!"

Of course, there were no mangoes in her fridge, no chutney to be made.

It occurred to me that here I was, back with all my former belongings, yet the whole time I was married, I felt caged and confined, fighting the role I was playing. Now and then I'd call Sally names and slam cabinet doors, basically kicking and screaming and storming out of the house with Howie at my heels. Off we'd go, driving to the pitch-black fields of Grassland Trail at midnight with Howie's dog tags jingle-jangling and his paws galloping over the grass.

Now I was home sweet home. Howie had come inside with me. I found him in Sally's bedroom on her sunflower bedspread. He invited me to lie down by stretching his tippy-toes and little black toenails all the way out, elongating his body so I could spoon him the way we used to spoon while waiting for Sally to come home. I checked my watch: two and a half hours to Sally.

So I rolled onto the bed with Howie and placed my arm over his rib cage. He smelled like he'd recently had a flea bath. I shut my eyes and felt a warm feeling in my chest. Howie rolled around to face me and draped his front leg over my waist. He looked into my eyes with his nostrils flaring.

And for a moment, Howie smiled—his gums pink and slippery, his tongue lolling over those itty-bitty baby teeth between long sharp canines. He gave me this look that was pure love. Breathing hard, his tongue quivered a little, and he stared at me with one ear cocked up like he was asking me a question: "Do you love me too?" My hand was on his chest, feeling him pant. As we stared at each other eyeball-to-eyeball, I couldn't understand why a woman had never looked at me like that, or how it was possible that a woman had never thrown her paw over my waist and snorted heavily and stared at me for minutes on end, wearing a huge grin, with her dark pupils dilated, her tongue hanging sideways out of her mouth.

Had Sally ever looked at me when I was emotionally naked and stared back with nothing but love? Had she ever let down her guard? Had she ever loved me at all? As for Howie, he refused to look away. It was the first time in months that I felt my body and soul were in sync, like I'd returned to the place where I belonged.

When I went back to my apartment later that night, I wrote about Howie in my *Book of Bad Ideas.* I wrote:

*Man's best friend
is his ex-wife's dog.*

A week later, the jig was up. Teresa came home early from the law office. It was lunchtime, and I'd been on one of those dates with Howie that always started out as an innocent walk but somehow ended up with us rolling into bed. I didn't hear Teresa walk in when she caught us frolicking on her white down comforter.

"Unbelievable," she said from the bedroom doorway. She'd taken off her strappy high-heeled shoes and held them in her hand like a weapon.

"You know," she said, and for a moment she put her free hand over her mouth like she might cry, like it was all too much to bear. "I think you're tragic."

I covered myself with a sheet and said, "I'm not tragic. You caught me in bed with a dog. This is comedy, not tragedy."

"You have no idea how bad this looks," she said. "I wish you could see yourself right now."

"Oh, come on. You're making a mountain out of a molehill."

She snorted in disgust. "Everything is a game to you. Just make-believe."

Howie was on his back with his back legs playfully kicking.

"Don't you play cute with me," she said to Howie. "Stay," she said. "Stay." Teresa put her shoes on the bed, then sat on the edge next to Howie. She grabbed one of his upraised paws and rubbed her thumb over the rough dirt-encrusted black pads of his feet. "Yeah," she said. "You like that, don't you?"

"Stop it, Teresa."

"What's the matter? Is this wrong?"

Teresa stroked her hand over his chest.

"That's enough," I said. "You'll get him worked up."

"I know what I'm doing." She found his toy bone on the bed and waggled it in front of his face. "I have your bone," she said in a sing-songy voice. "I have your bone."

"Would you stop?"

"I'm just playing with the dog," she said innocently. "This is how people play, isn't it?"

Then up went the bone, and she held it aloft like she was either going to throw it or brain Howie. Instead she said the one word Howie understood: "Out!" Howie shivered up from my side, stretched, jumped off the bed, and went brushing past her. That's when she said it again, to both of us, "Out! Out! Out!"

A divorced friend once told me that sooner or later my marriage would seem like blurry memories from someone else's life. Instead my marriage was a broken record of images that Sally and I shared together but interpreted differently. As I walked away from those moles in the snow that cold winter day, having felt the warmth of the mother's body in my palm, the dying heat of life, what I really felt was Howie's tragedy, not the mole's. Behind me, Howie had been pacing and whining and mourning his lost plaything. He was so upset I later bought him a new toy. Meanwhile, Sally had a white-mittened hand to her mouth. "Those poor babies," she kept saying. She said it thirty minutes later when we were back at the gravel parking lot. "Those poor babies," she said.

There was one memory I had, however, that Sally managed to dodge, one thing that defined our divorce: I stayed to watch our old cat Jojo die. It was the last thing Sal and I ever did together as man and wife—take Jojo to the veterinarian. The vet asked if we wanted to watch Jojo go down. At first we agreed that we'd face Jojo's death together, but at the last minute Sally broke down crying and backed out. So she stood in the hallway weeping, while I watched Jojo get pressed onto that stainless-steel table, hunkering down to avoid the needle in the back of her neck, squatting low on all fours, then twitching after the first shot, and thrashing like crazy to resist the second. Her claws scraped the metal table. A low growl emitted from her throat. Finally the doctor pressed her head against the cold table and forced the needle into her neck. Jojo gave me one last look, but it was a look that said nothing at all.

By the time the doctor called Sally in to see Jojo, the assistant had wrapped the cat in a clean white towel like a baby so only Jojo's sweet face showed. Seeing that cat, Sally let out a noise I'd never heard her make before. Not a shriek. Not a wail. But naked grief.

For some reason, I needed that image of death in my head. I needed to know what things looked like after the end.

• • •

Now it's fall in Columbia, Missouri, a new semester, a fresh start, yet for some reason I see Sally all over town. She's the lonely soul walking Howie through campus at night or the woman stepping out of a jewelry store downtown. So it's no surprise when I walk up 9th Street and see Howie with a big smile on his face and his tongue lolling out. He's tied to a bench in front of Lakota Café, and I bend down to scratch his neck. This is how it should be when ex-lovers run into each other on the street, all smiles and warm pats on the back. It's been over a month since I spent my last afternoon with Howie. When Teresa kicked us out, our summer had come to an end, and I returned Howie to his doghouse for good.

Through the café window, I see Sally sitting alone, so I walk in to pay my respects.

"You cut your hair," I say.

"I thought we agreed to be strangers," she replies. She's replaced her turtleneck with a tank top and gotten a bob cut. Her skin seems unusually tan.

Every time I'm face-to-face with Sally, it feels like we're still married, and a rain cloud bursts in my chest. "I want to talk."

"There's nothing to say."

"I want to talk about Howie."

She turns her head, and there it is—her bare neck—and I think: The back of your ex-wife's neck is a stranger's blank face.

Sally turns back to me. "Okay," she agrees. "Let's talk about Howie."

So I sit down and say, "You first. Why don't you ask about Morton?"

Her face softens. "Fine. How's Morton?"

"Miserable," I reply. "He yowls at night. He head-butts me when I'm asleep to get me to pet him. It's been rough."

"It's been rough for me too," Sally says.

She touches a silver dewdrop pendant hanging from her necklace. My eyes go to the blue veins mapping her chest, the fragile transparency of her apricot skin.

Then Sally says, "I've accepted that I'll never see Morton again." She nods and presses her lips together like she's about to cry.

Finally it feels like I'm winning a conversation with my ex-wife. "So," I ask. "How's Howie?"

"C'mon Hopper . . . don't you already know?"

For an instant I think I've been caught. Me. Teresa. The dog. The sordid scene of twisted bedsheets and drool. The two women—Sally and Teresa—meeting each other between their decks with their arms folded, nodding conspiratorially.

Sally's hand reaches out, not for my hand, but to grab the napkin on the table. She crumples the napkin to dab her nose and leaves it covering her mouth when she says, "I thought someone would have told you by now. He got hit by a car. Some stupid teenager . . ."

"Howie's sitting outside," I say. "Right on the sidewalk."

Sally shakes her head. "That's Joey, not Howie. It happened a while after the divorce. I didn't want you to know. I had to mourn alone."

I stand up and say, "I don't want to hear any more," refusing to consider the implications of me and a strange dog rolling in bed for two months. Before I leave the café, Sally puts her hand over her mouth and seems to convulse with grief, but for an instant, she might be laughing.

This is the last story I'll tell, a story from when I was a kid and had a sleek-haired black lab named Elvis, back when my family lived on ten acres of land where a dog could run free without fences or chains, just open country full of fleas and beggar's lice, and Elvis would come home with his fur crawling with seed ticks. Well, one day Elvis vanished, and we figured he'd gone girling around town. But he didn't come back, and there was no trace of him at the pound or signs he'd been rolled into a ditch. We figured he'd been killed, and a road crew had cleaned him up along with the deer and possum carcasses around town.

Six months later, that's when the Elvis sightings began.

First we heard stories that he was in a nearby neighborhood. Then friends called to say Elvis was running feral on Doc Saunder's farm. We heard a lot of other stories that didn't add up to squat.

My father left the same year, and we knew he'd gone off with some woman who lived in Independence, Missouri. Now Elvis was gone, and it was the only time I'd ever seen my mother cry. Well, when I heard Howie was dead, I felt betrayed and abandoned just like my mother had. Something in me wanted to die.

At the time of Elvis's disappearance, I was in junior high. Along with my mother's LPs of musicals, she had a stack of 45s from the 1950s. Most were Elvis Presley singles. My mother and I used to listen to the scratchy A-side of "Hound Dog," then she'd flip to the B-side's "Don't Be Cruel." The 45 was an old RCA Victor recording with the little black-and-white dog listening to a metal gramophone horn. I'd always associated that little dog with Elvis Presley's hound dog. I was just a kid then; I'd missed the whole point of the song. From then on, however, it was *my* Elvis that the song belonged to. *My* Elvis who made us croon "Don't Be Cruel."

The worst part of the whole story—the part I never told Sally or Teresa or anyone else—was that I never realized how much my mother loved Elvis until we found him on another family's couch. One day I spotted him on the walk home from my friend Joe Donnelley's house. Elvis was looking out another family's picture window. He saw me. I saw him. And I stood there calling his name as if he could read my lips through the glass. When I knocked on the front door, no one was there. I told my mother as soon as she got home from cashiering at the five-and-dime store. Well, she grabbed her purse, and we marched right back to that little white house with the blue shutters to confront the family who'd stolen our dog. "We've come for Elvis," my mother said to the gray-haired widow who answered the door. It was 1976. The King of Rock 'n' Roll was not yet dead. And the old lady got this look on her face, as if we were accusing her of diddling the King himself. "The dog!" my mother explained. "The black lab." Turns out the old lady'd renamed him Johnny Boy after she found him snuffling around her garbage cans. And no, Elvis didn't recognize us that day, not one bit. He just sat on that old lady's couch watching *Happy Days.* To Elvis, we were just strangers.

"Nothing good ever stays," my mother said, and that's when she went into the old lady's kitchen and leaned over a gold-flecked countertop to have her final cry. And no, Elvis never did come over to comfort her. And I didn't know what to do. And the old lady begged us to go. It all felt like the end of an era in our lives. I didn't even take Elvis home.

After seeing Sally, I sit at my computer to write about our conversation in my *Book of Bad Ideas.* So I write,

> *Dogs should run away*
> *but never die.*

But the words ring hollow, and I realize that running away is no easier than death.

I stare at the computer screen, still feeling torn up, when Morton leaps onto the desk to nuzzle me for affection. I push him away to type, then curse at him to leave me alone. But Morton keeps coming back to purr in front of the computer screen. And he keeps coming back for more love. No matter how much I ignore him, how much I push him away, over and over again, it's Morton who keeps coming back.

ANOTHER KIND OF SLEEP

1

Old Alexander Valinchuk lies awake night after night, listening to every noise in his tiny one-room studio—every creak in the floorboards overhead, every car passing on the street eight stories below, every door slamming shut in the hallway—but tonight, *tonight!*, after a small party in the neighboring apartment, an evening of tedious conversations, he hears someone outside his door. The knob turns, the latch bolt gives way, and his chest tightens like a fist. Fear makes him feel old. No . . . he *is* old, seventy-two, so old that he forgets to lock his door at night—and he's not only old but also weak in the heart. For fifteen years, since his wife's untimely death, Valinchuk has been beset with tachycardia—a racing pulse, tiny palpitations—for which he takes a handful of pills each morning with juice. At night, he lies awake, counting the ticks of his heart, bracing his chest with knurled fingers, feeling the one-two one-two beat. If he forgets to take his pills, his heartbeat races in the ¾ time of a Russian polka, and thoughts of death run together with boyhood images of his mother dancing to oompah music with visiting soldiers from the Russian army, boys in stiff uniforms who arrived late at night still smelling of pipe tobacco they smoked on the train.

Tonight Valinchuk's apartment door swings open, and his heart twinges with pain. Before he can catch a breath, the intruder fumbles for the light switch and flips it on.

Standing awkwardly in the doorway, seeming a bit dazed, is a woman, not a madman. Valinchuk can't help but laugh aloud, his heart beating hard. When he was mugged as a young soldier at a train station in Budapest, he laughed then too, but only after the thief had threatened him with a knife and demanded his money. He laughed the way people do when they feel they've escaped death, laughing as he explained to the police how the man pressed the knife to his throat and whispered a threat in Hungarian.

The woman backs up a step, on the brink of departing, blushing through her *so sorry*'s and *excuse me*'s.

Her chunky legs appear crooked in the yellow light from the hallway. Valinchuk wonders if this is the woman from next door who had been laughing loudly an hour earlier; he imagines her with her head craned back hard, her mouth wide open with teeth sharp against the air—that high-arched laughter full of smoke and booze. She is short, fiftyish, and wears a whorishly colorful skirt and an orange satin blouse. Matronly, but not quite—no, she is fending off matronliness by wearing dark panty hose and high heels, by perming her hair into frizzy ringlets.

"I thought you were coming to kill me," he says in a faint Russian accent. He laughs nervously in little *ho ho ho*'s.

"I couldn't hurt a soul," she says. "Well, I hope you can get back to sleep."

"I won't sleep." Valinchuk waves his hand dismissively. "I'm an old insomniac."

This woman would feel more nervous, more embarrassed for having walked in on this man, were she not a nurse. At the hospital she routinely walks into darkened rooms where sleeping strangers lie, usually her post-op patients in the post-anesthetic care unit and in earlier years her geriatric patients in the gerontology ward. What makes this room different is only the smell. What is it? Fried fish? It is a greasy aroma coming from a kitchen that abruptly cuts off the carpet with squares of linoleum, splitting the room in two: the bed on the one side, the kitchen on the other. It is a tight little apartment, much like her own studio, though hers has a squeaky hideaway bed behind a pair of shuttered doors. She has a couch and a café-sized dining set. The loneliness of her own tiny studio feels more familiar than this kind of loneliness. Here—in this man's modest room— is a kind of human hurt that has been left unmasked, naked, lacking tidy toss pillows to cover up the gloom.

She lingers in the doorway, eager to leave, and yet she says, "I know where the insomniacs go." She doesn't know why she has said this, but now the old man's long-jowled face is lit with curiosity. His milky eyes are poised on her, awaiting her next move. She idles for a moment, rests a hand on the doorframe. "They go to Café Milano downtown." She wants to be kind to him, seeing how he sits up with pillows heaped behind him. His bed is pressed too tightly against the wall where the party-goers next door laugh in a way that sounds feigned and desperate. She has the motherly impulse to straighten him, to unbend his knees and open his fisted hands, to move his body just as she moves patients so they won't get bedsores.

"Come join us next door," she says. "We can take a night journey to the café." Her voice is high and sincere.

"No. No," he replies. "It's inappropriate."

"Nonsense . . . what's your name?"

"Alexander Valinchuk," he says, then braces his palms against the mattress, shifting his weight to put his feet on the floor. "My friends call me Sasha."

Her name is Doris—Dorie to her friends but Dor to her mother and sister. She no longer knows what her name should be—Doris or Dorie or Dor. It used to be that she had many friends but only one name. Now she has few friends but goes by many names.

"Call me Doris."

She extends her hand and looks down at his round stomach. His undershirt dimples at his bellybutton. Valinchuk takes her hand not with a disingenuous, fish-slippery handshake but with a strength that surprises her.

He uses her hand to pull himself up from the bed, then says a little playfully, "Tell me, Doris, how is it that you know where the insomniacs go?"

2

This hand, this female hand with plump blue veins, is the second hand that Valinchuk has held today. Earlier in the evening, before closing the downtown library where he works, he came across one of the regular library patrons in the men's room on the first floor. He had given his key ring a vacant jingle that reverberated off the tiles, then knelt down on his good knee to look beneath the gray stall doors. Boots! Underneath the third stall, a pair of army-issue marching boots.

"Library's closed," Valinchuk said. "Clear out. Time to go."

Silence.

"This isn't a game. I see you," he said, then cautiously put his eye to the vertical crack along the edge of the door, thinking the door was latched shut, that he would have to coax the man out with kind words, but, no, the door had been left unlatched and swung open under the weight of his hand. There sat Simon, an elderly homeless man who ghosted in and out of the library. He sat cringing in the cold stall, his gray beard glistening with drops of spittle, his hands gripped around the black toilet seat beneath him.

"Take me home," Simon insisted.

"I can do no such thing," Valinchuk replied.

"Take me home," he repeated.

"Shhh . . . I cannot. Home is a place inside your head." Valinchuk tapped his scalp where hair had once grown in thick waves. "Here. Give me your hand."

Simon leaned forward, placed a scabrous palm in Valinchuk's, and hand-in-hand the two grown men walked out of the library, passing long study tables with green accountant's lamps and aisles of fusty-smelling books.

Now Valinchuk, in his pajama bottoms, holds a strange woman's hand. Releasing it, he combs his fingers through the thin, oily hair on the crown of his head.

"I must dress," he announces. Motioning with his hand, he tells her to turn around.

Valinchuk slides the cotton pajama bottoms down his old bowlegs, keeping an eye on Doris's round behind and wide hips. Why did he make her turn? He is too old for modesty, and yet not so old, not really so old. After all, he is still a man. Yes, a man, and from time to time he has urges, that irritating old itch, which he relieves every other month by dribbling his seed down the shower drain.

Once dressed, Valinchuk sweeps some loose change from the top of a bookcase into his free hand and places it into his pocket along with his wallet and keys. Of the sixty-some-odd books in the case, all of them are wrapped in sleeves of cellophane with tiny white stickers bearing call numbers on their spines. Some have bookmarks jauntily peeking from the pages. Doris's eyes are on the bookcase when Valinchuk turns to look at her.

"You like my books? They all have worms," he says and pinches together two stubby fingers to show her the size. "Little beige beetle larvae." He squints his eyes like he is trying to see a worm between his fingers.

"Are they old books?" She drops her eyes to the bottom level of the two-tiered bookcase.

"Not so old. Some books die young. Or should I say they get eaten alive? Yes, little maggots feed on them in the prime of their life."

It doesn't really interest her. Books. Dead books, no less. Or the living dead. Books about child psychology and heart transplant surgery and the Korean War.

"Shall we go now? Next door?" she asks and offers him the crook of her arm.

3

This party has clearly come to an end. Moody jazz plays in the background. Candles burn. Only two women remain, each holding a dark glass of wine. Ruth reclines against the toss pillows, restlessly tilting her glass to her lips, sipping. Her skin is oily with makeup and the flush of alcohol. Maude sits on the couch beside her.

"So you live in this building?" Maude asks Valinchuk.

"In 811," he replies.

Maude twists an unraveling thread from a blouse button; the fabric is tautly pulled and occasionally winks open when she inhales, exposing a fleshy burst of cleavage. Valinchuk looks away, inspects the apartment, which is the same as his. There is no place to sit, except on the floor, so Valinchuk and Doris stand awkwardly.

"You mean to say you live right next door? And yet I've never seen you! Isn't that funny?" Something cagey glints in Maude's smile. "Well, I'm so glad we've finally met."

"I, too, am glad." He lies. The truth is that Valinchuk has seen Maude's face denuded of makeup early in the morning when she dumps her garbage down the chute at the end of the hall. He has heard her on the phone, long after midnight, crying words into the receiver. Now she is in regal form. Skin powdery. Eyes purpled with liner. Hair full and enfrizzé.

Being invited to stay among these ladies would flatter him were it not for that fact that years ago Valinchuk had given up on women, stopped looking at them altogether except when young ladies stand in the aisles of the cramped evening bus, holding the overhead rail with their short skirts hiking up their thighs. He forces himself not to look, not to be tempted by a thing so trivial as sex. Even now, he feels a childish sense of shame blushing his cheeks in the presence of these women.

"We were talking about going to Café Milano," Doris says. "We probably should be on our way there right now." She suddenly wants to leave. Maude is too ghastly a sight, hideously single. Loneliness is such a garish emotion that Doris would gladly cut it out of her body, snipping it from the base of her soul like an inflamed appendix. Some days Doris regrets ever having divorced her husband, though she knew the relationship was dead when, one morning at breakfast, it occurred to her that they hadn't held a conversation in weeks, not a conversation that went beyond household pragmatics, and she sat there at the kitchen table, drinking coffee, holding a thumb to her emotions, until she couldn't stand it anymore and said, "Talk to me."

She still remembers the way her husband put his newspaper down, thoroughly galled. "About what?" he replied.

"What do other married people talk about?"

"They talk about their children. Is that what you want? Children?"

"You're putting words into my mouth."

"Am I?" he asked. He leaned back with his newspaper indignantly folded in his hand, then pushed away his plate of scrambled eggs before leaving the table.

"But I don't want children," she said to his back as he left the room. "This has nothing to do with children."

How she hated him at that moment, yet he may have been right. Yes, her complaint had everything in the world to do with children. Their whole marriage, her whole life, everything she longed for—somehow it has always been about children.

4

It is a short taxi ride through Chinatown to Café Milano, a corner café with big bright windows that enliven the dark street. At the chrome bar, a lone man sits in front of his laptop, typing. Two men sit at a window table playing chess while a third looks on. The onlooker stands up, and his chair leg scrapes across the floor. "You are afraid to take risks," he says to the players.

At a nearby table, Valinchuk wipes a grain of sleep from his eye and rolls it between his fingers for a moment. Doris self-consciously nibbles a flake of dead skin from her lower lip.

"It wasn't like this two years ago," Doris says, looking down at her coffee. "There used to be crushed velvet couches and Victorian lamps with fringed shades."

"It's not such a bad place."

"No? I'd hoped for something better," she says.

In this light, Valinchuk sees that faded red lipstick stains Doris's lips. Her laugh lines appear furrowed. He would like to see her put those lines to use, to see how her face must light up, how her gray eyes must gleam.

In Valinchuk's experience, there are two kinds of women—*curiosities* and *puzzles*. A curiosity merely arouses his interest, flashes and sparkles, but upon further inspection lacks an internal shine. A woman who is a puzzle, however, is someone he wants to study, to take her personality apart, each piece a geometric fragment—this piece is courage, that piece is severity, over here is a wedge of goodness, and over there is a block of suffering. And always, *always*, there are pieces that don't fit into any category at all, mysterious polyhedrons of personality that come rolling out when he begins to take the puzzle apart. Those are the women who drove him crazy in his youth. His wife had been a puzzle and remained a puzzle to the end.

This woman, Doris, she is neither a puzzle nor a curiosity but something entirely different, something that frightens him. He feels a need in her—a palpable need. The way she chattered on-and-on in the cab, asking him if he'd been married, how long, he hears tremors of self-consciousness in her voice. If he attempted to know her, God forbid, if he tinkered open the tight box of her soul, he might find another box inside. Boxes in boxes in boxes.

Doris leans forward, reaching for a packet of Sweet'n Low to pour into her coffee. Her cleavage shows. She would ordinarily pinch her collar together the way she instinctively does when leaning over patients in hospital beds, and yet she doesn't. "May I ask you something? About your insomnia?" she says, then rips open the packet. "What do you think about while you lie awake?"

"My life," he replies. "My mistakes."

She finds herself stroking her collarbone. Though physically he doesn't appeal to her—he is too old, too homely, not vital enough—there is an unconscious impulse to flirt. "I lie in bed and mourn for all of my past selves," she tells him, "the me of twenty who didn't know any better than to get married, the me of thirty who stayed married too long. It keeps going. There is the me of forty. The me of forty-five."

"After a certain age," Valinchuk says, "we all have stories in our souls that are slowly killing us."

"And what story is killing you?" She raises her cup to her lips.

Valinchuk takes a sip of his Turkish coffee. Thinking. Sorting through the memories. "Once," he begins, "back in the old country when I was a boy, an old woman came to our house and said that she had lived there, that she had fond memories of the place, and so my mother let her in.

The old woman peered through each doorway, then began to cry softly as she looked at the two priggish single beds in my parents' room, covered in tight French lace bedspreads that we'd inherited from my great-grandmother." He hooks a finger over his thick lips like a question mark and pauses, squeezing his eyes shut. "I remember the old woman wore a plain black dress like all Russian Orthodox widows. My mother made her some tea, and we sat in the drawing room where the old woman told us about her entire life, not just her childhood in the house, but about her marriage and the death of her husband twenty years earlier and about her son, a doctor who lived in Moscow. When she got up to leave, my mother embraced the woman, fondly, with the warmth of a parent—as though my mother were the mother to this senile old woman. And the two of them stood in the doorway, weeping."

Valinchuk drinks the dregs of his Turkish coffee. A trail of grinds runs up the edge of the cup and catches grittily between his teeth. He sucks them down contemplatively, then gives a shake of his head. "In our family, we did not even embrace our closest relatives. And we certainly did not cry in front of strangers. Yet for this woman my mother became large with emotions. Afterward, the old woman thanked my mother, and then she stood straight and thanked the house, saying, 'It is such a good house for a family, a wonderful house, a house full of love.' After that she went down the street with a rumpled kerchief pressed to her mouth. When the woman was gone, my mother came to me with tears still fresh on her face and said, 'Sasha, do not tell your father of this. Understand? That woman never lived here. Tomorrow she will go to someone else's house and say she lived there. And the next day she will go somewhere else.'"

After telling his story, Valinchuk stares into his small empty cup. Doris thinks of her own stories, her own agonies. She wishes she could tell one story, just one story of her life that redeems her, a story that will make anyone who hears it say, "Yes, Doris, you *are* a good person. You deserve better. You deserve to be loved." But she can think of no such story. Her work as a nurse certainly has redeeming qualities, yet it's her job, her profession; she is nothing more than a medical mercenary going from door to door with a dosage of false cheer and a small cup containing analgesics to relieve the pain. Of her failings and flaws there are many stories.

"Now you must tell me your story," Valinchuk says.

"I don't think I have one."

"Of course you do."

"I can't think of one specific story. I can only remember the dozens of small stories that rattle around in my brain."

"Then tell me one of those."

"They aren't as good as yours."

"Just tell something. This isn't a contest."

"Okay. I have one story," she finally says, "but it happened in a dream. I dreamt that I went into the hospital one night, when all of the patients were sleeping, and one by one I put my hand on their foreheads and healed them. They each sat up, fully recovered, and thanked me. Then they all started to walk out of their rooms, and I realized that in healing them I'd become sick with their emotional ailments. While they shambled down the halls in their cotton gowns, I crumpled to the floor. Then one of the doctors saw them leaving and yelled, 'Stop! You are all very sick! Go back to your beds.' And they did, completely forgetting that they'd been healed. They all went back to bed and shut their eyes. And now I was the sick one, without a bed, twitching on the floor. Isn't that awful?" She smiles painfully after telling the story. Her hand rises to cover her mouth. "It's a silly dream. I don't know why I told it."

"I'm glad you told it," Valinchuk replies.

Finishing the last of her coffee, Doris rests her cup on the table and looks out the window, out beyond Chinatown where buildings come into view. Among these buildings appears the white sign of the hospital where Doris works. The night nurses are on duty, the interns come and go, foggy post-op patients in the post-anesthetic care unit roll upon waves of anesthesia. Every now and then, a post-op patient wakes blearily into a room full of other sleeping post-ops, realizing that he is alone and in a strange place, that he has been drugged, that his body has been opened and that tumors have been ripped out. Doris's face is usually the first face such patients see. She must remain calm and loving and kind; she must explain where the patient is, why he is there. Most post-ops are sore and want to go back to sleep, so she coos gently, saying she'll make the pain go away, and increases the drip until the patient has receded, slipping back into the peaceful ether, and when the patient is ready to wake he gets wheeled into a private room, never recalling the post-anesthetic care unit or that it was Doris who alleviated his pain. Maybe, just maybe, her life is redeemed in these forgotten moments.

"Listen," she says, resting her hand on Valinchuk's, then drawing her middle finger across the coarse hair above his knuckles. "I should get home." She looks into Valinchuk's face. His eyes are warm, not handsome, but warm.

5

They take a taxi back to Doris's apartment on the east side of town, sitting silently, listening to the dispatcher on the cab driver's radio. Doris grazes Sasha's leg with her knee. They look at each other—*she,* as if to apologize, and *he,* smiling, pats her hand on the seat between them. He gives her fingers a brief squeeze before releasing them, enough to make her heart leap in her chest. *There it is,* she thinks. *There it is.*

Her apartment is in a tall brick building with a sickly little lobby, empty except for its wall of mailboxes. The elevator, cranky and old, opens its doors haltingly to deliver them to the tenth floor, where Doris leads the way to her studio, smiling back at Valinchuk as she inserts the key and opens the door, letting him in.

Valinchuk lingers in the middle of the room, looking around her rosy little world, feeling out of place. Not knowing what he wants here, if he wants anything at all, he stands while she takes off her shoes. She pulls down a hideaway bed with jangling and popping springs, then sits on the edge rubbing her toes through her panty hose.

Doris wishes they would touch. Instead Valinchuk places hands in his pockets and shuffles around the room, looking at photos. She wishes touching were easy, the way it is with children: you see a crying child and pick it up.

"I'd like you to stay," she says, worrying that he has come all the way to her doorstep, all the way to her bed, and will leave her lying painfully awake. Doris watches his face as she unbuttons her orange blouse, waiting for him to acknowledge that she has made her move, wanting his ugly mouth on her neck and breasts, wanting him *because* he is so ugly, because an ugly man, she thinks, will love her harder and longer, will savor her more than one who easily gets what he wants. Her blouse drapes open to expose her black bra underneath. She reclines now, casually leaning back on her elbows. Waiting. The entire moment a gaping wound.

"I should go," Valinchuk says.

Doris sits up and clutches his thick fingers. Valinchuk feels his heart shrink; it is a child's heart, fragile and small, beating fiercely.

"Sleep with me," she says.

When had they agreed to have sex? Valinchuk thinks. He had sensed no silent plan, no secret agreement. Yet here he stands, an old man, with an erection comically saluting his sexuality. He wants nothing to do with it. He will not have sex. Not because he is unable, but because he has trained himself not to need it, not to want it, not to look for it in the slow-eyed old ladies who flirt with him when he is vulnerably climbing the library's ladders to retrieve books perched high among the stacks.

Looking at his face, so hideous, Doris thinks she can't bring herself to do it. Sex is not what she wants at all. Sex is merely a pretense to touch him, to put her arms around him; her desire has nothing to do with intimacy, and everything to do with sanity. "I mean *sleep*," she says. "The other kind of sleep. Not sex. Fall asleep right here in this bed."

"I can't."

"Of course you can." She squeezes his hand. It is a tight, desperate grip.

This is some kind of trick, he thinks, a sinister seduction. First sleep, then sex. He will not be duped. His wife died fifteen years earlier, and she was the last woman he'd slept with. He had never known how to make love to her. Always something went wrong. She was too dry, too uncomfortable, and made painful grunting noises when he tried to enter her. Their old bodies had no rhythm. She refused to take off her nightgown and made him pull it up over her hips in an effort to hide her gray pubic hair and bloated stomach. Loving her had never been easy or spontaneous or natural. Sex was so complex that he once dreamt his wife had a round keyhole where her vagina should be, and that he was on his hands and knees looking for the key while she sat on the edge of the bed with a red dress raised over her thighs, her thick legs spread open, inviting him in, but he could not enter. Not without the key! Now he was too old to get down on his hands and knees only to find another woman's locked-up sex organs.

"Just sleep here beside me," Doris says, grasping his hand with both of hers. "Let me hold you. My God, that's all I want."

Valinchuk thinks of his mother, how she squandered her affection, loved recklessly, had sloppy affairs when he was a boy, how he listened to her moan in the tiny bedroom beside his. Afterward she'd make tea for whichever lover she'd been with, all of whom she called "doctors," though they never carried a doctor's case nor prescribed her medication. His mother and the doctor would stand in the kitchen, sipping tea and talking too loudly, both of them thinking that the boy—Sasha—had been fooled. Only in hindsight had he figured it all out, during long nights of insomnia when he pieced together the truth, and the truth was that, yes, his mother's house had been full of love, the old widow had been right about that much, but it was not pure love; it was the love of an order that he wanted nothing to do with. His mother was sick. She wanted to be a mother for everyone— for every man who used her body, for every old woman who wandered into her home on a gray afternoon.

"I cannot sleep," Valinchuk says.

"I have pills."

He shakes his head. "Pills don't help."

"Just try one. Please . . ."

Valinchuk frees his hand. "I should go. You have been very kind, but I should be going."

He backs away from her, then turns rapidly, clutches the doorknob, and leaves.

Doris lies awake on the bed, wounded, feeling cut open down the middle. She stares at the webs on the ceiling and recalls the last time she felt something akin to love. God, it caught her by surprise. The man, Joseph, was nothing more than a post-op patient whose leg had been amputated. After tending to other patients she noticed Joseph's sheets were pulled down and his cotton gown was raised over his bare chest, exposing his genitals, as though he'd wakened briefly and searched for his missing leg. He was a young man, young enough to be her son. When Doris found him, he was sleeping, sedated. She leaned down to the dark blond hair cupped over his ear, and maternally said, "Joseph?" No response, no sigh, not even a flutter of his thick eyelashes. He would have radiated health were it not for the stump of his leg. She began to pull his upraised gown over his naked torso, and the side of her pinkie finger, just the knuckle and tender meat between the joints, grazed against the muscles on his chest. As she pulled the gown over him, she let the side of her knuckle slide all the way down his pectoral muscle, over the tender peak of his nipple, down the emaciated cup of his stomach, and over his thigh, until her finger stroked the gauze wrappings and hit the air of his missing leg. Touching him gave her a tender thrill, so sexual and yet so motherly. She wanted so badly to touch him, to lay her hands all over him, to wrap him in her arms and love him. The next day, Joseph was gone, moved to a private room, the entire moment never felt by his anesthetized body.

Outside Doris's apartment, there is light. Still awake, she hears a radio droning. A garbage truck stops in the alley and hydraulically wheezes as it lifts each Dumpster. Glass bottles clangor and shatter. Somewhere an alarm clock goes off.

THE TIKI KING

It's Sunday again, errand day, which means dad puts his cell phone in his sweatpants pocket, and off we go to the hot tub supply store or Radio Shack. We get stuck behind a slow '80s Monte Carlo on Olive Avenue. That's when dad says he's figured it out: "Burbank is full of old men with no place to go."

Last week dad said Burbank was Hollywood's ugly stepsister, a plain Jane town with pancake-flat streets, not many curves, and hills in all the wrong places. When I replied, "Yeah. . . so?" dad said, "Yeah . . . so?" except his voice was nasal and whiny and supposed to sound like mine, but it didn't.

We drive by the Safari Inn, a '50s-era motor lodge with a huge neon sign of a yellow tribal shield and spear. Palm trees and stucco buildings line the rest of the block. The Safari Inn stands out like some crazy abandoned movie set, like it belongs in a bad Elvis flick.

When dad starts talking again, I daydream about entering the sixth grade at Valley Alternative, a magnet school near my mom's office in Van Nuys. It's June, so I've got nothing to do all day but watch satellite TV, play Final Fantasy, and run errands with my parents. Mostly I think about girls. Sometimes I daydream about what it feels like to be in love. To kiss a girl. To look intensely into another person's eyes and somehow care about them. Except I don't know a single girl worth caring about.

"You know," dad says. And I can already hear what's next: dad's figured something else out. "Burbank isn't even Apple Pie America anymore. It used to be Apple Pie, if you know what that means."

I know what it means but can't bring myself to respond. All I want to say is, "I know all about Apple Pie America, dad. I know it's Joe DiMaggio and Superman comics and backyard barbecues and the American flag on the moon. In other words, it's a lot of stuff I don't really care about."

We're stopped at a red light and our turn signal blinks eight times before dad says, "Burbank is more like chess pie. Your grandma used to make chess pie each Christmas. You know what chess pie is?"

"No."

"It's all the brown custard you get in pecan pie but none of the nuts." The light turns green. Then dad says, "Hollywood has all the nuts."

"Tsss," I say and shake my head.

"Tsss," he replies and shakes his head.

In my bedroom there's a huge poster-sized aerial photograph of Burbank. I found it the last day of elementary school in Mrs. Garcia's garbage can. It's black-and-white on thick paper that's yellow around the edges. A razor-thin font below the photo says, BURBANK, Ca. 1961. The year my mother was born. I like the way the streets line up straight and squared at right angles, except Olive, which cuts a crazy slant all the way through Burbank. And I like how the homes look like Monopoly houses, like I could pick them up and crunch them with my back teeth. But what I like most, more than anything else, is how Burbank makes sense from up high more than it does from down below.

The next weekend, mom and I run errands in Toluca Lake, a community next to Burbank that looks like a crappy town from the '50s. The first thing you see in Toluca Lake is a giant baby-faced Bob's Big Boy statue holding a hamburger up high on a plate. All the storefronts have canopies with the store's name on them. Some places have old neon signs, the kind they flash in lame movie montages when small-town characters in '50s films arrive in the Big City to start their new lives. Except none of it is exciting like the movies make it out to be. It's all boring stuff like Papoos Hot Dog Show and Patsy's Restaurant.

"Sometimes I feel like I'm back in Kansas," mom says. We're at a stoplight on Riverside Drive. "Everything is so bland and practical. Not that the Midwest is bland, really. It has its charms."

Mom's an insurance adjuster, which means she works a lot of overtime and holes herself up in the home office most weekends. During the week, I'm not allowed to stay home alone, so I have to hang out in her cubicle until summer camp starts. She sits next to a woman who wears too much perfume and makes personal phone calls to a man named Pookie.

After driving through Toluca Lake, mom takes me to a dry cleaners in Studio City that has a wall plastered with 8½ by 11 headshots. When I was five years old, I first noticed headshots in restaurants along Ventura Boulevard. One day when I saw headshots at the carwash on Alameda, I asked dad, "Who are all these people?" We were standing in the hallway with long windows where you watch your car get washed. Behind us was a wall covered in photos. In front of us, black plastic strips slapped suds on our SUV. Dad turned to look at the headshots behind him. "All these people," dad said, "they're all idiots. That's who they are." But it turned out they were just actors, not idiots.

Inside the dry cleaners, there are so many photographs that there are headshots on top of headshots, and they're all actors I've never heard of. Sandy Smith. John Treedle. Valerie Newman. Most of them are just the face of some person who's either smiling or looking artificially serious. I scan the walls expecting to see my own face, the face of an aspiring star, even though I don't aspire to be anything at all. Instead I only see faces of happy women with fluffed '80s hair alongside men who don't smile at all.

A couple of years ago I was in our garage and found a box of headshots of mom, except it wasn't mom. She had this other name, this other life. Her name was Julie instead of Jane. And her last name was Aster instead of Aronis. She looked like a toothpaste ad—broad smile, straight hair, bright eyes. Trees filled the background of the shot. I kept staring at the picture of this innocent pretty girl with long caramel-blond hair, repeating the name in my head. Julie Aster. Julie Aster. After a while I put the picture back because it felt like I was looking at my mom's dead twin, as if Julie Aster were some girl that nobody wanted to talk about, this secret person we kept tucked away in a box.

My mother's hair isn't caramel blond anymore. It's dirty blond or dishwater blond, one of those ugly blond colors from a bottle of Clairol. While my mother is pulling out her checkbook to pay for the dry cleaning, I scan dozens of pictures on the wall for Julie Aster. I'm pretty sure she isn't there.

About once a month dad gets me in the car to run errands, and we end up driving by his childhood home in Burbank, a few miles north of our current home, close to a bunch of electrical transmission towers by the airport. All the streets are flat, just like our own neighborhood. Dad always drives real slow with one hand on the steering wheel while he looks out at the homes. And dad is always seeing something that I don't see, cause sometimes he gets real pissed off. "Look at that," he'll say. "They haven't mowed the lawn in three weeks. Nobody takes care of their shit anymore." Then he'll speed off, hitting the accelerator too hard, and he'll stay angry for the rest of the day.

"Dad," I once told him, "You don't live there anymore." He didn't answer, so I said, "Dad, you've got a family of your own."

So today when he takes me to his old house, he says, "Look. Look at that." A *For Sale* sign sits in front. It's a white stucco Monopoly house with an oil-stained driveway, just like every other house on the block. Small. Ordinary. For a moment I think no one special or particularly smart could have ever lived there.

Dad pulls over to the curb and parks.

"What're we doing?" I ask.

"We're gonna check things out."

I get out of the car and follow dad around the side of the house to a wooden gate leading to the backyard. Dad reaches over the top of the gate, fiddles around, and un-latches it. Inside there's an empty pool and a small patio with salmon-toned concrete. No grass. No landscaping rocks. Instead of grass, the edge of the house is landscaped with green spiky ice plants that are wet inside like cactus. I break off a spike of ice plant and write "Nobody lives here" on the hot concrete. Cinder-block walls border the yard; one has a nasty crack that looks like the letter Z patched over with white cement.

Dad goes to a window and cups his hands around his eyes to see inside. He waves me over to look into the house. I see a crappy-looking room with wood paneling and a rug that's pulled up to show the grainy hardwood underneath.

"I bet they want three-quarters of a million," he says. "And my old man bought this place for ten grand." He turns and walks down the kiddie steps of the drained pool into the deep end. The lining of the pool is robin's-egg blue. Dad looks like a freaky hatchling down there, standing in a half shell in his sweatpants and sunglasses, looking up at me like

I'm supposed to feel whatever it is that he feels—something for the house, something for the pool. But it just feels like a stranger's backyard to me.

"Son of a bitch," dad says. He shakes his head like there's something going on in his brain that I don't really want to know about.

When he sits down on top of the leaves at the bottom, I say, "Dad, you're gonna get dirty."

"Tsss," he replies. And then he says, "I almost drowned in this pool."

"So?" I say.

"I almost drowned," he repeats.

"So?" I say again. "What's your point?"

"That's exactly my point," he replies.

He stands up, brushes off the leaves, then climbs the deep end's ladder until he's standing across the pool from me with his hands on his hips.

"Right here where I'm standing my old man had a giant tiki statue, and all the landscaping along the walls was filled with palms and tropical plants. And at night, my old man would come out here after work, turn on some tribal drum music, light some tiki torches, and sit back on a lawn chair drinking Mai Tais, not saying a damn word. He'd just sit stony and silent each night. The rest of us would be inside watching *Gomer Pyle,* and he'd sit under the patio umbrella with a hand to his brow, staring out at the pool."

"Dad?"

"Yeah."

"Why are you telling me all this?"

"Because I played along. I brought him drinks in plastic cups shaped like coconuts. I got him Hawaiian shirts for Father's Day." Then he looks at me and says, "You know what the problem with you is? You don't know how to play along."

I suck in my cheeks, insulted, but I don't know why I should feel insulted, cause I don't even know what playing along means in this situation. Am I supposed to jump into the empty pool? Supposed to break into the house?

"Humor me a little," dad says. "Can't you at least do that for your old man?"

"I don't know what you want."

"Act like you care."

"I *am* acting like I care."

"Then you're a shitty actor," he says.

"Whatever," I reply and kick around some leaves on the patio.

Dad paces around the pool and says, "Every weekend, my old man became the Tiki King of Burbank. But on weekdays he was one of these button-up types who worked over at Lockheed Aircraft and wore horn-rimmed glasses and looked like all those guys in the control room at NASA in the '60s. Like the guys that put Neil Armstrong on the moon."

Dad puts one foot up on the diving board and grabs the aluminum handrails.

"You know what we did on weekends? My old man would drag me and your Uncle Mike to a store called Akron that had all this tacky Polynesian crap, and that was our big family outing, going to Akron and shopping for bamboo furniture and ashtrays shaped like conch shells."

"Yeah?"

"Yeah," he replies. "All right. Let's get out of here."

When we get home, dad comes up to my room where I'm sitting on the floor and makes me stop playing Final Fantasy to shove a photograph in my hand.

"See?" he says.

It's an old-timey black-and-white picture with a fluted edge, a picture of Grandpa wearing a skinny black tie and a short-sleeved white business shirt and black horn-rimmed glasses. His hair is dark and combed back. And he's resting his right elbow on an evil-looking wood man with a mouth shaped like a sideways 8 that's screaming and has little carved round teeth. Behind him, I can see the pool and a few bamboo torches that aren't lit. And there's a patio chair with someone sitting in it, but you can only see legs crossed at the ankle. A woman's legs. She's wearing heavy black shoes with a chunky heel and a skirt just at the knee. For some reason, I can't stop looking at those legs.

"Can I have it?" I ask.

"Why?" Dad's drinking a Coke. He takes a sip, then looks over the top of the glass.

"Just because."

"What're you gonna do with it?"

"I'll put it up on my wall."

He looks over at my map of Burbank. "Why?"

"I don't know," I say.

"I don't think you should have it."

But he doesn't take it back. So I keep it anyway. Just because.

Sometimes when I'm watching old movies on weekends, I see a girl in the background who looks like Julie Aster. She's sitting in a high school cafeteria with her shiny caramel hair down the length of her back, shyly eating a sandwich. The next week she's the girl on a college campus who walks toward the screen and looks out through the camera straight at me like she's about to say something important, but just when she opens her mouth to speak, she turns her face away. One time I saw her in that old movie *The Paper Chase*, so I sat there reading the credits at the end of the movie, searching for her name, but it wasn't there.

I keep Julie Aster's headshot in the top drawer of my desk, not on my wall with the map of Burbank and photo of Grandpa. On the back of the headshot, Julie appears in a series of small photos. In one she's holding a daisy and wearing bell-bottom jeans. When I first found the box of headshots, I thought she was in her mid-twenties, but now I think she might have been closer to my age, maybe fifteen or sixteen, some girl I might have met thirty years ago in Apple Pie America, a girl off a Greyhound bus from Kansas, a girl in a pink bikini at the pool of the Safari Inn. Maybe even a girl who was waiting for Elvis.

When I close my eyes, sometimes I want to run away with Julie Aster. I want her to push the hair from my ear and whisper, "Let's hop on a bus and go." The possibilities are endless because Julie Aster is adventurous. She's not afraid to stare straight at the camera, not afraid to hold my gaze. Except Julie Aster is also my mother, and I don't want to go anywhere with mom. And the truth of the matter is that there's not really anywhere to go.

The next weekend dad drags me around Burbank to run errands. We go to Pep Boys with the cartoon faces of Manny, Mo, and Jack on the top of the building. Then we drive to Toluca Lake, and I sit in the car while dad goes across the street to The Money Tree. When I ask if The Money Tree is a bar, dad says, "No, it's a joint. Burbank is full of joints. Not bars."

He makes me wait in the car for twenty minutes without the radio, so I sit there playing my GameBoy until he finally comes out.

When we get home, mom has taken a break from the computer and is in the kitchen drinking a glass of water.

"So where'd you two go?" she asks.

"Some joint," I say.

Mom raises an eyebrow. "What kind of joint?"

"Some money joint."

"Oh."

The next weekend dad says we have errands to run, but all we do is drive back to his parents' house and park. Now the sign says, "Price Reduced."

This time dad gets out of the SUV and tries the front door. It's locked. A key box is hanging from the knob. "Son of a bitch," he says. He gets out his cell phone and calls Uncle Mike in Florida, and I just stand there on the oil-stained driveway looking up at a basketball hoop that dad and Uncle Mike might have played ball at. There's an old '70s photo of dad with Uncle Mike on top of our entertainment center. Uncle Mike's got his arm around dad like they're best friends back home from the war. Instead of wearing dog tags, they're both shirtless and wearing gold chains around their necks. Dad has this bushy brown mustache and sideburns and a head of curly hair. He looks way too toned and tan. Now dad is heavy, with no mustache, and he wears sweatsuits every weekend but never works out.

Dad is still on the phone, so I roam the tree-lined sidewalk. When I look down the block, all the homes look the same to me, the way they look from my aerial map, homes side-by-side and back-to-back with little concrete patios and kidney-shaped pools fenced off with brick walls you can't see in the photo, but you know they're there. All the neighborhoods are cut into grids as if God decided the world should be like this, linear and cloned, like the end of that book *A Wrinkle in Time* when the characters enter an alternate universe where there's a neighborhood of identical houses, and all these kids stand in all the driveways bouncing balls in sync. Somewhere inside an aerial shot of Burbank, I'm one of those kids who's supposed to be in sync. Except I don't even own a ball.

When dad gets off the phone, he starts prowling around the house. He walks to the shrubs under the picture window and digs. "Look what an idiot your Uncle Mike is," he says and holds up a fake rock. Inside the rock is a house key from twenty years ago, maybe more.

"It won't work," I say.

"Shut up. It'll work."

He goes to the door, and I can't believe it, but it works.

"See?" he says. "You stay out here. Holler if anyone's coming."

He shuts the door behind him. It's the kind of door with three little rectangular windows lined up like steps near the top. I have to stand on my tiptoes to see inside. I hear dad get back on the phone with Uncle Mike. He sounds mad.

When dad comes back out, I ask, "What'd you see in there?"

"Nothing."

"Were you looking for something you'd left behind?"

"Yeah."

"Did you find it?"

He says, "No," then puts his hand over his mouth and chin like he doesn't want me to read his lips while he thinks out loud.

We get back in the SUV, and dad's still got his hand over his mouth. He looks at the basketball hoop in the driveway. Finally he looks at me and says, "We should play basketball sometime."

"I hate sports," I say.

"How could you hate sports?"

I shrug my shoulders. "What's so great about baseball or basketball? I don't get it." The truth is that I'd always faked liking sports. I faked it when we played flag football. I faked it the year I was in Little League. Basically I'd been faking it all for years.

"Kids are supposed to like sports. What the hell is wrong with you?"

"Nothing's wrong with me," I say. "I'm normal like everyone else."

On weekdays, I'm stuck with mom at work. Some days mom gets busy, so she puts me in a lunchroom with a long table and microwave. Ladies from the office go in and out with cups of coffee and bags of popcorn. I sit there with my Game-Boy. Sometimes I bring a book.

Today two of the office ladies come into the lunchroom together while I'm reading the *Los Angeles Times.* Except I'm not really reading it. I'm just flipping the pages looking for comics like *Ballard Street* and *Bliss.* One of the office ladies says to me, "Hey kid, you seem real mature for your age." There are thirty people who work in mom's office. Some of them talk to me, know my name, ask about school or what I'm reading. Some don't. Instead they ignore me like I'm not even there. This office lady is one of the people who always ignores me. She's blonde with big front teeth and drinks her coffee with lots of powdered creamer. Her friend must be new. I've never seen her before.

"How old are you, anyway?" the friend asks. She's wearing a blue skirt that hikes above her bare knees, and I can see the goose bumps on her legs.

"None of your business," I say and feel myself smile inside, cause I'm just starting to realize there are a lot of people in this world that I don't like, and these office ladies, they're just the beginning.

"Come on. How old are you?" the friend asks.

"Don't talk to him," the blonde with big teeth says. "He's a smart-ass. Probably takes after his dad."

"Shut up!" I say.

"No. You shut up!" says the blonde with big teeth.

Now I'm in trouble big. They're gonna tell mom. But by the end of the day, if they've told her, mom never says a thing.

Dad's a tax analyst for Chevron. He commutes to work in El Segundo. An hour and a half each way. He gets home after eight if traffic is bad, then watches HBO or sports. Tonight, after dad's settled in, he takes control of the TV that I've been watching and flips the channels until he gets to a show called *Kojak.* The opening credits are running.

"Dad. Change it," I say. "I don't want to watch some stupid old show."

"I've worked my ass off all day, and you won't let me watch a little *Kojak*?"

"Can't you watch something else?"

Dad gets this serious look, and I know I'm in for something.

"Don't change the channel," he says and goes into the kitchen. I hear him dump ice into a glass. He opens a can of Coke, and the ice jingles before he walks back into the living room.

"Did I ever tell you about the year your Uncle Mike decided to be Kojak for Halloween?" he asks when he sits down.

I thought I'd heard all of dad's stupid Uncle Mike stories, but this one I've never heard.

He grabs the remote and mutes the TV. "When your Uncle Mike was sixteen, he shaved his head bald and sucked on lollipops and walked around saying, 'Who loves ya, baby?' cause that was Kojak's line. 'Who loves ya, baby?' You following me so far?"

"Yeah."

"So anyway. After Halloween, the whole thing backfired. Mike got food poisoning. Lost a lot of weight. His hair didn't come back in right away. Then everyone thought he had cancer. For a month, friends would walk up to him at Gilbert's Five-and-Dime saying, 'Oh my god! Oh my god! When did you start chemotherapy?'"

I start to laugh. Uncle Mike is a big guy now. Over two hundred pounds. He's this rich developer who lives in Orlando, Florida.

"Don't laugh. This isn't a funny story. You know the saddest part of this story? It was your grandma who had cancer, and nobody knew it. Your grandma . . . my mom.

Well, Mom used to smoke Virginia Slims and sell Avon to old ladies in the neighborhood. She'd wear this green eye shadow and cruise around in her El Dorado with a cigarette hanging from her lips." Then dad turns to me and says, "Me and your Uncle Mike, we didn't get Mom. With our old man, we tried to understand what he was going through. But with Mom . . . well . . ."

He looks at me hard at the end of his story and says, "What's the matter? Aren't you gonna ask me, 'What's your point?'"

"No."

"Why not?"

"Cause I get it, dad. I get it."

He shakes his head like he doesn't believe me. It's like he's disgusted.

"What'd I do now?"

He presses his lips together and says, "Never mind." Then he un-mutes the TV to watch *Kojak.*

"What?" I ask. "What'd I do?" I'm beginning to get mad. No matter what I say or do, it's always the wrong thing.

"Idiot," dad says. "Your Uncle Mike was an idiot."

I sit there with my arms folded, not saying anything.

Lately when dad and I run errands on the weekend, he says we're going one place, but we end up somewhere else. Trips to the post office become trips to his old house. Last week a trip to RiteAid became a trip to The Blarney Stone. Today we take a trip to Vons Supermarket that becomes a trip to The Money Tree. He leaves me alone in the car. The sun's beating through the SUV window onto the green plastic dashboard. Both windows are rolled down. There's a hair salon a few doorways from The Money Tree and women come and go.

I forgot my GameBoy and after twenty minutes, I can't take it anymore. I lean over the driver's seat and yell out the window, "Dad!" I'm hoping he'll hear me through the joint's open door. "Dad!" I yell. But nothing happens.

That's when I get the bright idea of getting out of the car and going in. After crossing the street, I walk over to the open door. "Dad?" I say and stand there blocking the sunlight.

Inside there's a bar on the right and red vinyl booths on the left. Dad is the only guy in the joint. Just him and the bartender. Dad's sitting on a barstool with a can of Coke in front of him. I wait for one of them to notice me. I feel like a giant standing there. All five feet of me seems to tower over the joint and cast a long shadow down the red carpet.

Finally the bartender looks over and says, "Hey kid, come on in." He waves me over with his arm.

The only light inside is coming in through the door. The air smells like stale cigarette smoke, and I feel like I've traveled back to some shady Frank Sinatra era. I pull out a barstool by dad, but just as I sit I get this bad feeling. Dad still hasn't turned to look at me when the bartender puts a bowl of shelled peanuts on the bar. The bartender looks at dad, as if waiting for a cue, before saying, "Alright, kid, name your poison."

"Gin and tonic," I reply.

He starts making a drink, tossing ice in a glass. Then he works below the bar and sprays the soda sprayer. The whole time dad's not doing anything. He's just sitting there with his elbow on the bar and his hand on his forehead like he's sick. The bartender gives me my drink with a wedge of lime on the side.

"To your health," he says. Then he rests both hands wide apart on the bar, arms open. His posture makes me think of a priest, like I'm supposed to fess up to something I did. Except I'd be fessing up to doing nothing.

"Your old man here is on the wagon," the bartender says.

"What's that supposed to mean?"

"It means he stopped drinking three months ago."

"I'm not an alcoholic. That's not what this is about," dad says, but he's still not looking at me. He's taken his hand off his forehead and looks beyond the bartender. "I'm just not gonna drink anymore. That's all."

"If you're not an alcoholic, but you need to stop drinking, then what are you?" I ask.

Bottles of Beefeater and Smirnoff sit against a gold-veined mirror behind the bar. Dad stares out at his reflection between the bottles and sucks his teeth. "I'm bored," he finally says.

When he turns to look at me, I can see lines around his eyes that appear deeper in the dim light. I'm not sure what to say. My dad is bored. It doesn't really seem as bad as he's making it out.

"Well, I'm bored too," I say.

"I know," he says. "I know."

"Maybe we should get a dog," I say.

"We've already got a cat."

"We could go on vacation. We could go to Hawaii."

"We can't afford it. We've got too much debt."

I take the first sip of my drink, and it's so bitter that I almost spit it out. It tastes like tonic and 7-Up.

"I'm not just bored," dad says. "I'm indifferent. I feel nothing. I have no passion. Stan, what are you passionate about?"

The bartender smiles. "Jazz," he says. "And my wife."

"What does it feel like?"

"Hell, I don't know. It just feels good."

Dad's got me thinking: What if I have no passion? I've already spent my life driving in circles, waiting for something big. What's gonna become of me when I'm fifty years old and that big thing never happens? It scares me, and I take another sip of gin and tonic.

"What about you, kid?" dad asks me. "What are you passionate about?"

"I'm only eleven," I say.

"You think that's an excuse? *I'm only eleven,*" he mimics me in a high nasal way that doesn't sound like my voice at all, as if he's reminding me that I'm still a kid. Except he rubs it in my face, and it doesn't really seem fair. "Well, you've got another think coming, cause I was eleven once too." His voice has that ugly edge to it, the same edge it gets when he comes home from a bad day at work. "*I'm only eleven.* Is that all you can say?" Dad throws his money down and pushes away from the bar. "Well, you know what? I've had enough of eleven. Sooner or later, you have to grow up." He drains the last of his Coke and looks over at me, his face pulled down with anger.

"Why are you looking at me like that?" I ask.

"I'm not looking at you like anything."

I swallow hard, and he's still looking at me, his facial expression like Grandpa's tiki statue.

"What did I do?"

"It's what you always do," he says. "Always the same fuckin' thing."

I hop down from the barstool. "Fine," I say. "Can we go now?"

"No, I'm not done. Sit the fuck down and wait like you're supposed to."

"All I ever do is wait." I can feel my face getting red as I stand there.

Dad's grimace deepens, and he says, "Sit the fuck down!" Now his voice is fire hot.

I'm standing on the red carpet, and the sunlight from the open door is hitting my arm like a sideways spotlight. I can see my own shadow casting down through the bar. And I can tell by the way my shadow is getting long that the angle of the sun is getting lower, going down.

And I'm about to sit when I realize that I don't have to. I can say *No* if I want. None of it really matters. No one really cares. Nothing has consequences.

So I take two steps back and say it. I say *No*. Except I say *No* in the worst possible way: I tell my old man to fuck off. And you know what? It feels good in a bad kind of way. Liberating. "Fuck off." When I say it, I feel it too. I feel something ugly curl inside of me, like a huge worm that's been coiling in my chest has finally woken up.

Outside the door people walk by. A motorcycle drives down the street. If I were looking at this bar from up high, it would actually look all right. Safe and distant. Just a boxy little building. Nothing I couldn't crunch with my own back teeth. But inside the air is thick. And dad's face is a giant twisted fist. His nose curls down like a beat-up boxer. He gets off his barstool and takes three steps toward me in slow motion. Then he stops and looks at me hard. "Mr. Fuck You can find his own ride home," he says and jabs me in the chest with his index finger.

"Fine," I say. My heart is pounding, and I can still feel the spot between my ribs where his index finger poked me.

Jabbing me again, he says, "I'm gonna be just like you from now on."

"Good," I say. "Great!"

"Cause I don't give a shit about anything," he says as he stomps past me. "I don't give a fuck." Now he's standing in the doorway with his arms folded in front of him.

"Just go," I say like I don't care at all. "Get out."

The bartender is staring at me. I can tell he's waiting for me to stop dad, but I'm not about to budge. We both watch him leave the bar. And it's the weirdest feeling in the world watching dad go to the SUV. I watch him drive off, leaving me inside the bar alone with the long shadows.

"Well . . ." the bartender says, his voice rising. And I say, "Yeah . . . ," except my voice drops.

"Shhhh . . ." he says, like he's about to say *shit*. "You wanna call your mom?" he asks.

"Sure," I say, cause I mean, can it get any worse? What's worse than being eleven years old and having your mom pick you up from a bar?

"He's been jerking me around all week," I say to the bartender, shaking my head, then drinking my gin and tonic.

The bartender puts a black phone in front of me. It's an old-timey phone with a round dial and an earpiece that attaches to a spiral cord. I'm not even sure if I know how to use it.

"Here," the bartender says. He takes the earpiece off the cradle and shows me how to hold it. I can figure out how to dial on my own.

"Mom?" I say when she finally says hello. Her voice is sleepy like she's been working on the computer all afternoon. "Dad and I got into a fight."

"Oh yeah?" she says, and I can hear things in her voice that I definitely do not like.

"Can you pick me up?"

"Yeah . . . sure." Again, she's got this thing in her voice where she drags out the *yeah* too long. It's like she's almost laughing at me.

"I'm at a joint called The Money Tree on Riverside Drive."

"Is that what they're calling The Money Tree these days? A joint?"

"Yeah," I say. "A joint."

Thirty minutes later, mom walks into the bar wearing jeans and a sleeveless blouse. Her hair is pulled into a loose-knotted bun with strands softly falling out from the back. She looks single when she sits on the barstool beside me. I'm pretending to watch a Dodgers game on TV. She orders a merlot, looks at her watch, and we sit there, not talking. I can feel her presence tapping her fingernail against the bar. And I can smell her papaya shampoo. Suddenly I feel like the type of loser in a bar who wants to talk to a woman but can't, like some lame TV character that makes bad jokes and embarrasses himself. When I look at the side of mom's face, she's looking up at the baseball game, and Vin Scully has just announced a third strike. For an instant I can tell that once upon a time, mom was beautiful—like Julie Aster—and that somewhere along the line, probably because she had me, she's grown less and less beautiful over the years.

"What?" she asks, then looks over at me kind of angry, and I can't tell if she's joking or serious.

"Nuthin'," I say.

"Right. I bet it was nuthin'." She shakes her head, looks back at the TV. The bartender puts her merlot in front of her, and she takes a long drink.

I want her to be my mom and take me back to that place where we were a family that did fun things. Instead she says, "So . . . you and your dad got into a bar fight?"

"Sort of."

She nods. "Had he been drinking?"

"No."

She nods again, then says, "Your cat's gone missing."

"Yeah?" I say.

"Yeah." Then she tilts the glass to her lips again, and I think that any minute now some man is going to enter the bar and whisper in her ear, "Let's hop on a bus and go." And that maybe she'll leave me here forever. I get this image in my head of living the rest of my life in a bar, just a kid condemned to wash highball glasses and sleep on vinyl booths with cigarette burns in the seats. I want to tell her that I don't want her to go away. But how do you say something that isn't even real in the first place?

She finishes her merlot and finally looks at me, and I see now that her mind has been elsewhere, just off in a world I know nothing about.

When we get home, dad's still not there. Which is a relief. It gives me time to get out and look for the cat in the

neighborhood. Half the homes on our street have new owners who work for Burbank Studios or Warner Brothers or
Universal or NBC. None of them have kids I can play with.
It's not like five years ago when my best friend lived two
homes away. I don't feel comfortable knocking on doors,
because the Cardinelli family is gone and the Martinez
family is gone. There are six *For Sale* signs up and down the
block. Some of the signs say *Foreclosed.*

"Kitty," I call out, but I'm not feeling what I'm supposed
to feel, not what I felt when our cat Ringo went missing six
years ago. Then I cried and cried and mom held my hand
and walked the neighborhood with me. Tears ran down my
face, and Mrs. Alberty and the two Cardinelli boys came
out of their homes. People stopped and talked to us and
promised they'd search for Ringo. Now it's just me looking
for a cat with no name, a cat I don't even care about, a cat
dad probably backed over with his SUV. But I have to go
through the motions cause it seems like the right thing to
do. So I walk up and down the block, feigning emotions for
a cat I don't love, hoping a neighbor who's never met me will
open a door and invite me in.

I don't go home until I think dad's had enough time to
cool off. It's dusk outside when I walk into the living room.
Mom's upstairs on the computer. I go into the kitchen for a
glass of water and through the window over the sink I see
dad in the hot tub. Our yard is small. The hot tub is pushed
against a cement-block wall. Dad's eyes are shut, and his
arms are stretched over the rim of the tub. Then he opens
his eyes and glares at me, and it's one of those looks I'll carry
around for months, a look that says I'm the bad guy in his
life, as if I've always been the bad guy, and he's just now figured it out. But from where I'm standing, I'm just a normal
kid. Bubbles percolate around him like boiling water, and
it all puts an image of a backwards fairy tale into my head
where the kids put their parents in a soup pot and boil them

until their flesh falls off the bones. And then the kids eat the soup, but it doesn't make them full. So they keep eating and eating until their parents are gone.

A few days later it's the Fourth of July. Which feels wrong, cause it's a Wednesday but feels like a Saturday. Mom and dad both have the day off. Dad is watching a Dodgers game, and mom is upstairs working. Before dusk, mom finally comes down from her office and says, "Let's go see fireworks. Just you and me."

We drive through the Valley, past the glitzy restaurants and shops of Ventura Boulevard. Mom cruises up the hills to Mulholland Drive where she pulls over at an unmarked lookout point. We sit there, above the San Fernando Valley, looking at the world through our windshield. From high up, you can watch an entire string of stoplights, miles of them, turn from green to yellow to red. They all change in unison, which you can't tell from down below, where it all feels chaotic and random, like the lights change whenever they want. From up here, everything looks orderly and predictable, the way God would want things to look.

"It looks just like it used to look when I was young," mom says. So we sit there, watching the grid of lights and twinkling Valley below. Our home is down there somewhere by one of those faraway looking stoplights. And we're up here like the kings of the city with nothing to do but look down.

Mom takes off her seatbelt and starts talking. "I used to come up here with boys who drove their parents' convertibles," she says, "and we'd sit and talk about our futures with so much optimism. And sometimes we would kiss, but it was innocent, not dirty or sexual. Just kind of sweet."

I look away. My eyes fall on her bare legs where her skirt rests above her knee. The idea of mom kissing boys puts a bad image in my mind.

Out of the blue she says, "Give me a kiss," just like when I was a little kid and she'd turn toward me at a stoplight, move my bangs out of my eyes, and say, "Kiss me."

But I'm not a little kid anymore and say, "Mom. That's weird."

"I don't mean it in a weird way. Just give me a kiss. Right here." She taps a hollow spot on her cheek. "C'mon . . . it won't kill you to give your mother a kiss."

I'm about to say, "No," but she looks so disappointed that I lean over the stick shift to kiss her. Half of me is afraid she'll turn her mouth and force me to kiss her on the lips, afraid that her whole face will turn toward mine and her eyes will be open and that we'll have to face each other like that—too close, too intimate—that we'll have to connect lips and stare into each other's eyes. Julie Aster's eyes. Eyes that won't look away.

But she doesn't even look toward me when I pucker against her cheek. I can smell her lipstick as I pull away. It's the kind of awkward kiss that's full of forced familiarity, like the kisses I give my Great Aunt Louise at Christmas when I thank her for a new sweater.

"Gee," mom says, touching the spot where I'd kissed her. "Is that it?"

"I guess so."

"Thanks," she says, but her *thanks* is as fake as my kiss. And when I look at the side of her face, she looks just like the office ladies she works with.

When I turn toward the flat streets of the Valley, all the lights change in unison from green to yellow to red. We sit and watch, saying nothing, just waiting for the fireworks to begin.

GEISHAS

1

If Laurel's mother were still alive, she'd call it smut—an ugly, contemptuous word punctuated by a hard "t." Her father would have playfully called it burleycue because of the town's strip club, the Old Burleycue, a name full of deception, conjuring old-time cancan dancers, not topless local girls from last year's Homecoming float.

Smut. Burleycue. Neither term captured the bitterness of finding her husband's porn magazine three months after he'd gone missing in his work truck. Laurel couldn't casually roll it into a joint and smoke it like the pot she'd found in his sock drawer. There was no way to make it her own.

After thirteen years of marriage, she'd grown to accept that her husband masturbated to images of other women, accepting that other men might even masturbate to her image, maybe the sixth-grade teacher at the elementary school where she taught or the acne-scarred Wal-Mart clerk who flirted with her in the checkout line. All a woman had to do was give a man a bump—a tiny flirtatious gesture—and she could get that man to walk away thinking about her. Laurel was thirty-three, still slender and cute. She could give a man a bump if she wanted to, but all she really wanted was for her husband Wakefield to come home.

Before finding her husband's porn stash, Laurel had been soaking a sponge in Lysol, cleaning the base of the toilet to sanitize the house for the arrival of her brother-in-law's eighteen-month-old son, and there it was—the edge of the magazine, a small triangle of pages, the rest of it wedged behind the toilet tank. She tugged at the corner, and it dropped to the floor, opening to images of skin and feathers and blond hair fanned over black satin sheets.

Down there with the curly hairs, Laurel sank into the damp nook beside the toilet and flipped through the magazine's porcelain-cold pages, forcing herself to read it, imagining her husband's freckled back arched over each airbrushed nude body. In all her life she'd never been naked like those women, naked but clothed in persona.

That afternoon she sat on the bathroom floor reading the article about a married man who enjoyed the services of prostitutes during his business travels to Tokyo and Taipei, girls educated in the secret knowledge of sexuality. All were performers trained to serve men, to be perfect women. And they weren't geishas either—that was a misnomer. Real geishas were entertainers, not prostitutes; some danced, some sang, some merely served men's meals. Not even geishas knew exactly what they were. To Laurel, it made no difference—all Asian prostitutes were geishas. She thought about telephoning her sister to say, "Have you and your husband talked about geishas? Isn't this a talk we should all have? Shouldn't we get it out in the open?"

2

Outside a storm moved over the sky, pushing along like a dark barge up the nearby Mississippi River. Laurel watched her brother-in-law Dan pull into her driveway, scraping the underside of his SUV over the mohawk of weeds in the median. Next door, the Dangler home was empty, left unsold when Mrs. Dangler died. Ivy climbed its walls and vines grew over the windows.

"So they tore down the old five-and-dime," Dan said when he entered Laurel's house. Miles, slung on his hip, blinked sleepily, sucking his thumb.

"We go to the Wal-Mart in Hannibal now," Laurel said and took the oversized balloon-print bag from Dan's shoulder.

Dan was already walking through the hallway to a small room with a single bed and a fern in the window. "And Snoozy's ice cream parlor?" he asked.

"Gone too."

"Jesus, nothing's left."

"Well . . . nothing but me," she said.

Dan came to visit from Saint Louis once a year, out of familial duty, with birthday presents mixed in with Christmas gifts. She'd known him for fifteen years, and yet she didn't know him at all, not in the way she knew her sister's husband. Wake's family had always been secretive and polite, nodding and smiling, holding the world at arm's length.

She stood beside Dan while he set Miles on the edge of the bed. The child wavered, sitting upright. Dan removed the boy's shirt from his sticky chest.

"By the way," Dan said. "Miles likes to sleep without pajamas when it's stuffy like this." He maneuvered Miles onto his back to thumb the fabric of his overalls over his bulky diaper. The boy's eyelids fluttered; he made a moue of complaint. "Sometimes he takes his diaper off during the night. He's between diapers and potty training. I hope that's not a problem."

For a moment she softened enough to feel motherly as she watched Miles sleep. Before her husband left, Laurel imagined she and Wake might someday stand over the crib of their own child feeling a boundless kind of love. Love for the child. Love for her husband. That moment never happened, and now Dan, still wearing his business clothes, played the role of the dutiful daddy and tucked Miles in. Laurel touched the boy's sweaty cheek. Dark bohemian curls fringed his ears and forehead, so much like her husband Wake's head of untamed curls, and unlike Dan's, whose hair was short and receding. From certain angles, Dan looked just like her husband—same square jawline, same long nose. She wanted to reach out to touch Dan's cheek just as she'd touched Miles's, but touching was a forbidden thing. It was okay to shake hands with strangers, but she couldn't lay a finger on an extended family member. A fragile emotion broke like an egg inside her, a happy sadness. Here she was in this perfect moment, feeling married to Dan, like newlyweds with their firstborn child. It was Wake, not Dan, standing by her side, Wake's affection for the child that she saw in his eyes, Wake's soft cheek that she wanted to touch.

Dan turned from Miles, caught Laurel gazing at him, and his delighted expression wilted. His hair was cut so short that it brought out the veiny streaks in his eyes. Smaller and narrower, Dan was a balled-up version of Wake, a sickly stand-in. Nothing like Wake at all, she now realized.

Dan knelt down, rummaging through the boy's bag of diapers and clothes. "Sorry about this last-minute overnighter." He dug through the bag and pulled out a furry green turtle. "We just found out the sitter has chickenpox yesterday."

Standing, he placed the turtle in the crook of Miles's arm and brushed some curls from his forehead.

"Miles is wonderful," Laurel said. "That little wife of yours must have Fabergé eggs in her ovaries."

There. She'd reclaimed a piece of herself, a bit of her dignity. Unfazed, Dan looked at his watch. He hadn't even changed from his work clothes before swinging into her home with Miles, as if seeing Laurel were business, the last chore of the day, something to slash from his To Do list. She was beginning to suspect that this whole idea of spending the weekend with Miles wasn't a playdate and that there was no babysitter with chickenpox, no outbreak of chickenpox at all. This was an emotional errand.

3

Laurel was raw, Dan thought. He could tell by the tone of her voice. She looked good, though—young and slender—but not muscular like the secretaries at his office. This diet of grief had improved her figure. If he hugged her, he could fold Laurel in his arms like a bird, feel how fragile she was. When his wife Irene's flesh pressed softly against him, he thought of something that should be set free.

Dan never really understood this lifestyle of Wake's, how his brother put up with being married to a school-teacher, how he worked as a dairy-truck driver. Wake could have gotten an MD or a PhD. He'd scored high on IQ tests. Dan had set his sights on big things for Wake—the way he read books, stacking them around the bed at night, how he hitched rides from Angora to Hannibal's public library with Mr. McKinley, his high school English teacher. Later, when Dan got his license, Wake hitched rides with Dan, even when Dan was on a date, just to get to the library's air-conditioned reading room. Those were the best times they had—driving down Old River Road, the windows down, the dusty smell of clothbound books on Wake's lap. The road snaked around steep, craggy bluffs overlooking the Missis-sippi River. Sometimes they'd stop at the lookout points to stare down at the water, feeling the awe of that river and the peace of knowing that civilization could come to an end, and the Mississippi would still be there, visible from outer space, a jagged line marking Home on a map.

The adult version of Wake was an enigma to Dan. The teenaged version made more sense, even if Wake did pull a few vanishing acts—one day here, two days there. Still, he always showed up with a grin on his face like he'd been play-ing some trick on the family, some twisted game of hide-and-seek. It was all a joke to him.

Dan felt certain that Wake was just fine. It was Laurel who concerned him, her well-being, her state of mind. His own brother had done her wrong, and Dan felt responsible, guilty, as if he'd been the one who'd driven Wake into oblivion. "What if Wake never comes back?" Dan's wife asked while lying awake in bed, their bodies separated by a ridge of heaped sheets. Dan told her that this was just a game Wake was playing, that he always came home. "What if he doesn't this time?" she replied. Two days later his wife concocted plans for Miles's visit with his Aunt Laurel.

Laurel turned out the bedroom light. Dan, checking his watch, wanted to go home. Mind your own business, he thought; that would be best. Being alone with Laurel made him nervous, self-conscious, like he was sixteen again and incapable of stopping a blush.

"Are you going to rush off?" she asked. "Or would you like to stay for a drink?"

"Sure," he said hesitantly. "How 'bout some beer?"

Inside the kitchen, the air smelled antiseptic, everything overly clean. Through the window over the sink, dark clouds smudged the late evening sunlight, and overgrown grass swayed in the wind of an approaching cold front. Dan paced the linoleum, picking up odds and ends: a group photo of Laurel's first-grade class standing toothless and proud, a miniature milk-jug magnet, a business card stuck to the refrigerator that read Martin Thorn, Detective, Angora Police Department.

"That detective's an idiot," Laurel said, turning as she took glasses down from the cupboard. "He calls once a month to say he has no new leads. We went to high school with him. Remember? He would have been six years younger than you."

Dan looked at the name again, shrugged, shook his head. "He would have been twelve when I left for college."

Laurel sucked in her cheeks. "Half the people in town can't look me in the eye," she said. "Then there's the other half, guys like that detective. And that detective seems to think he and Wake were great friends." She opened a cabinet and brought down a dusty bottle of bourbon. "Wake couldn't stand him. These so-called friends keep coming out of the woodwork, trying to comfort me." She rocked back on her heels and looked Dan straight in the eyes. "I don't buy it for one minute."

Dan put the card back under its magnet. "We could hire a private investigator."

"Wake'll come back."

"I hope so."

"I know so," she replied. "Wake's pulling a stunt like that guy in London who left his wife for years, then suddenly returned."

"What guy was that?"

"Oh, God, some guy back in the Victorian era. Anyway, he was living a few blocks away the whole time."

"Wake could never get away with that in a town this small."

Laurel let out a huff. "It's just a story, Dan. Sit down." She chinned toward the table, then walked over with the bottle and glasses. "We don't have beer. Just bourbon."

"That'll do." Dan sat, pushing a box of mail to the table's center.

Laurel settled into a director's chair and shot a cold smile at Dan, a smile that felt like a kick in the groin—no teeth, just dry pinched lips. Dan poured Laurel a two-fingered glass of bourbon, then poured a glass for himself.

"Just so you know," he said. "Miles might get separation anxiety. Anyway, if Miles gets cranky, sing him a kiddy song."

"Like what?" She eyed him over her glass of bourbon.

Dan thought for a second. "I usually sing this jingle that me and another pharmaceutical rep came up with." He picked up his bourbon and coughed after taking a drink.

"Go on. Sing it," she said. "I'm curious."

He hated doing anything for an audience. Even after a shot of bourbon, he felt like a goofy kid on a stage. "You're going to think it's stupid," he said.

"Just sing it."

"Okay. Here goes: This little pill makes you happy . . . This little pill makes you calm . . . This little pill makes you disappear . . . Poof! And you're gone."

Laurel clapped her hands. "That wasn't so bad."

"Miles is crazy about the 'Poof!' part," Dan said. "It cracks him up every time. You have to make a big show of it, like it's a big surprise. POOF!" He waved both hands in the air. "Go on, say it. POOF!"

She shook her head. "I can't."

"You're no fun."

"I'm plenty of fun. You're just trying too hard."

Dan took a long drink, nodding. "Well, I thought you might need a laugh."

Laurel emptied her glass and smiled. "I thought the last little pill went *wee wee wee* all the way home."

Now she laughed, and it was a nice long roll of exhales that made her chest heave up and down in her tank top. Dan smiled in return, feeling that a tiny door had opened, and she was going to let him in. This wasn't his brother's wife anymore. This was a woman with fragile green eyes and a loose breathy laugh. Dan drank the bourbon to soften himself, to see if he could find the nerve to let the door stay open.

"You look good," he said. "Like you're holding up."

"I suppose I should be falling apart, right?" Laurel perched an elbow on the table and placed her fist under her chin.

"You're strong," he said. "I always knew you were."

She looked at him squarely, suspicious. "I'm fine."

Perspiration dampened Dan's neck. He tugged at his shirt, then unbuttoned the top two buttons. "You know what gets me the most about Wake's departure? The middle-class paradox: Everyone wants to walk that line between freedom and security." He lifted his glass and drank. "I always thought that Wake was exempt from all that."

4

Laurel cradled the glass in the ball of her hand as she turned Dan's last comment over in her mind: Wake was exempt from all that. What was that supposed to mean? A tiny star of anger, just a pinprick of velvety heat, blossomed in her chest. She poured another shot and drank till the burn in her throat mellowed. She drank to calm the frayed feeling that was coming on. Already she could feel the bourbon glide through her body.

This was the first conversation she'd had face-to-face with Dan since Wake's disappearance, and he was just as bad as everyone else: he didn't know what to say, so the wrong things came out.

"I don't think I understand," Laurel said, trying to remain cool. "What would Wake be exempt from?"

"Wake seemed content. That's all." Dan looked at the window and the growing darkness outside. "He never complained."

"He was extremely content," she replied. The liquor had jiggled Laurel's personality. She fidgeted with the box of Wake's unopened mail that sat on the table, drawing it toward her, then placing it on the floor. Now only the bottle of bourbon stood between them. "Christ, when was the last time you spoke to Wake? A year ago?" She looked at Dan's sweaty upper lip.

"Listen," he said. "If anyone were to run away from his life, I thought it would have been me. That's what I meant."

Suddenly Dan felt he'd said too much and wanted to swallow the words back. Instead, he poured more bourbon into his glass even though it wasn't empty. For Wake, it was easy to walk away from it all, that's what he'd wanted to say. What did Wake have to lose? No kids. No investments. No 401(k). If Dan were to walk away from his life right now, he'd lose everything. The job. The house. The stock portfolio.

Laurel was smiling straight at Dan, pinched and unwavering, a smile she held so long that he didn't know what to think. His brain flashed the image of kissing the bourbon off her lips and sliding his tongue against her teeth. That would put her in her place, he thought. He batted the image away. For Christ's sake, she was his sister-in-law. He longed to be as pure-minded as he was when he first married Irene. During their first six months of marriage, only his wife's image floated into his mind, then other women started buoying up at irregular intervals. Such thoughts would go away for a few weeks or maybe a month and come back again. Dan saw images of himself with bank tellers and office temps. He never knew when the next one would surface.

5

Laurel looked down at the table and rubbed her nose with the knuckle of her index finger. Her hand stank of the inside of a polyurethane glove. She was dirty all over—dirty from perspiration, dirty from cleaning fluids, still wearing the dirty running shorts and tank top she'd cleaned the house in. Bon Ami faintly powdered her arms and legs. Her ponytail, coming undone, released curls around her ears.

"I won't run away from Irene," Dan blundered.

"You might." A gay cruelty came over Laurel. She had his secrets, and she thought about Wake, his secrets. She poured herself more bourbon. "Did you know that Wake read porn magazines?" she asked.

"No."

"Do you read them?"

"I don't make a habit of it," he replied.

Dan raised his glass and drank until it was empty. When he lowered his hand, he let his tumbler hit the table with a hard wooden knock. The kitchen windows rapped gently from the wind. Dan looked at the leafy vine climbing the glass—all gray outside, except for the fluttery leaves, as if the ivy were growing in around them and sealing the house shut.

"I found some porn behind the toilet today." She leaned down to Wake's box of mail on the floor. "Here it is. Seemed like something I should save. I didn't want Wake to come back and get mad at me for tossing it out."

She flipped from image to image: an all-girl beach party gone wrong, one topless girl squeezing suntan lotion onto her girlfriend's back. The pictures seemed less painful to look at now, less like smut and more like the harmless girlie magazine that it really was.

With bourbon, Dan thought, all rules of decorum had slackened. Anything goes, that was the feeling he had. They were entering into a relationship with an unknown code of conduct. He was no longer her brother-in-law and not her drinking buddy either. Whatever tiny door had opened earlier that evening, it was now locked shut behind him; another smaller door had appeared, and here he was, without the key, trapped between the two.

Laurel sat with one foot on the chair and hugged her bent knee to her chest, not a position she would sit in at Christmas dinner on one of his mahogany dining set chairs, nor the way she would sit if Irene were present. Irene would slap Dan on the knee if he dared place a foot on the coffee table or couch. She didn't even like it when he sat around with his shirt off. His bodily oils, Irene said, would damage the couch's fabric.

Laurel leaned over the table and turned the magazine pages to one of the nudes, a girl on her hands and knees with big breasts dangling down like a cow udder. She was half-costumed as Wonder Woman wearing the gold bracelets and headband, except the gold Lasso of Truth was coiled and gripped between her teeth.

"This girl." Laurel pointed. "Look at her. How old do you think she is? Sixteen? Seventeen?"

"Eighteen."

He turned his eyes away. It was wrong to look. He wanted the image out of his head. Less than a year ago he was getting a routine physical, a complete workup, and he wanted to ask the doctor if there was any way to stop himself from thinking about women. He was pondering it just as the doctor put his cold fingers around his testicles, thinking that there must be some pill to get rid of stray thoughts, when the doctor said, "Have you noticed this? This here. A lump." The doctor grunted in a way that sounded serious. "A lump?" Dan asked. The doctor grunted again, the timbre of his voice darkening, saying nothing of cancer, not yet, only saying, quite seriously, "A lump."

"Would you leave your wife for a girl like that?" Laurel asked.

"No! For Christ's sake, Wake didn't leave you for another woman."

"That's not what I think," she interrupted.

"Then why?" He put out his hand, stopping the direction of conversation. "Never mind. Whatever went on between you two, it's none of my business."

"Nothing went on." Her voice was high.

Dan kept his mouth shut.

"It's true!" she exclaimed. "We never argued."

6

Then Laurel told Dan about the last bad argument she and Wake had, the time they argued so fiercely that Wake slept in the yard under a green canvas tent he'd picked up at an army surplus store. In the morning, Wake roped open the door flap and squatted in front of a propane camping stove where he made coffee, dumping clots of powdered milk into the warming brew. This went on for an entire week. He on the outside. She on the inside. Neither one of them speaking to the other. Wake would get up at dawn and make oatmeal and coffee in the morning haze. Laurel watched him through the kitchen window while she washed dishes or buttered wheat toast. If he happened to notice her there in the window, he'd wave and nod as if she were a curious neighbor. She was fine with it. Really fine. Even in the wretchedness of their worst domestic dispute, Wake always did something playful to amplify the silliness of feuding.

The argument occurred during the last recession, when the population of Angora went below five thousand. This was after the hospital moved its facilities to Hannibal. Both houses on either side of theirs were vacant. Wake had the whole yard to himself—privacy, emptiness, no neighbors peering out of windows or mowing the lawn. It was summer, hot, so after breakfast Wake would strip naked, turn on the garden hose, and wait for it to jump to life in the middle of the yard. He'd wriggle a stream of water under his arms, over his hairy chest, and down the white rivulets of his scalp. The curly hair on his body darkened wetly against his legs and chest. After bathing, when he was getting ready for work, Wake didn't bother to put on any clothes. He was slender then, and muscular in the arms and thighs from lifting dairy crates.

In the end, it was his easy nakedness that Laurel remembered most vividly, the way he made it look so natural to walk around the backyard nude. He'd hose off his dirty breakfast dishes naked and shave naked in the reflection of the sliding glass window. By 7:00 a.m. he'd put on his blue work pants, then walk alongside the house to his truck in the driveway.

On his last morning outdoors, Laurel caught Wake pissing on the lawn. No clothes. No shame. He leaned back on his hips and made a glorious arc. She then realized Wake had become a different man. All those years, she'd known him only in the context of containment—within walls, behind doors. Out in the open, he was untethered, feral; nothing from society was left on his skin.

"Then one day Wake came back inside," she told Dan. "And he didn't say a damn word. He was sitting in front of the TV with a Coors in his hand. It was all a big joke to him. So I don't see why he couldn't be in a shady RV park with a generator hooked up to the dairy truck. And when he's good and ready, he'll turn up on the sofa in front of the TV like he'd been sitting there all along." She raised her glass to her lips, then tipped her head back to finish the bourbon. "Anyway, if you'd known all that, maybe you wouldn't be here to check up on me."

She refilled her glass, then went back to the magazine, turning to the next image. Another page. Another woman. "What do you think of her?" Laurel asked, pressing her finger onto the page.

"I'm not here to check up on you," Dan said. "I'm just here to drop off Miles."

"Really? You don't like her tits?" She held the magazine over her chest and looked down at it, trying the breasts on for size.

7

Dan glanced up when the first pinging of rain hit a tin ventilation duct over the stove. Suddenly a harder rain drummed overhead, and darkness filled the window over the sink.

Dan felt disoriented, fogged by the bourbon. He looked at his watch. "I promised to help clean the house before the trip," he said. "Every weekend Irene's got me busy with chores."

"Before you leave, tell me, how would you like to fuck someone like that?" Laurel held up the magazine.

He refused to get flustered. "Laurel . . . ," he began, his voice begging her to stop.

"I'm just asking," she replied innocently.

He looked at the picture. In truth, he'd never cheated, hadn't even come close. No woman let him get beyond deep eye contact. When he was young, some juvenile fear struck him down at even the stab of eye contact with a girl. Not anymore. Now he liked to hover near the reception desk at work where the young women who answered the phones laughed so readily. Irene had stopped laughing like that. There was nothing lighthearted when they argued, nothing that could be made into a joke. Irene held grudges. At a moment's notice she could rattle off a list of indiscretions— parties where Dan overeagerly filled another woman's wineglass, nights he stayed out too late with the sales team after work—all innocent improprieties. He tried to make light of them, which only made things worse.

Dan was suddenly conscious of the silence in the kitchen, just the sound of rain outside. No TV was running. The refrigerator shifted into a hum. From the other room he heard his son's high shallow breathing and felt the smallness of the boy's lungs, the constriction. Music—Dan wanted music, noise, distraction. It made him uncomfortable, this tight emptiness.

"You haven't answered me," Laurel said. "Would you sleep with this girl?"

"No." He paused. "That kind of question isn't appropriate."

The first four months after the lump was discovered, after the orchiectomy and cancer treatment, Dan underwent blood tests, had radiation therapy, took antidepressants. His probability of being cured was 99 percent. And he was cured—all thoughts of other women vanished.

8

Laurel laughed out loud at the thought of appropriateness, at the entire idea that decorum or rules existed. Decorum was for that abandoned wife in Victorian England, not Laurel. The magazine sat open in front of her. Here was decorum. Here were rules. One rule for your wife, another for your lover.

Laurel turned the page. "You know what's funny about this? About all these naked girls? What's funny is how unreal the poses are. The first time I saw a magazine like this, I was just a kid, six or seven, and I was at my friend Maya's house. She'd stolen the magazine from her older brother's room and was really excited about it. She wanted me to undress and do things like that." Laurel pointed at the picture. "When I refused, Maya said that if I wouldn't do it, then she would pose for me, so she took off her clothes, not all of them, she left her underwear on, and she did some of the easy poses." Laurel paused for Dan's reaction. He looked only mildly surprised. "After one or two poses, Maya and I both started laughing at how ridiculous it was, how silly the poses looked when you actually tried to do them. Then again, Maya was really good at it. She could do things with her eyes and lips. She'd been practicing."

Laurel had never been any good at moving her hips or doing a striptease. Too stiff, that's what her high school dance instructor told her. A little bourbon on an empty stomach had loosened her up. Now it would be easy to strike a pose. Butt out. Back curved. Boobs high. Perhaps that had been her failure as a woman and a wife: she was too domestic, not sexually entertaining.

"Look." She stood up. Taking her hair out of its ponytail, she tousled it with both hands until it straggled over her shoulders. Her tank top strained against her breasts. She put her hands on her hips and thrust out her chest.

Dan sat there with his hand clenched around his glass of bourbon.

"That's pretty good," she said. "I couldn't do anything like this when I was a kid." She posed again with her butt out and her arms crossed like an X over her breasts. "Look how easy this is. Wake doesn't know what he's missing."

Dan covered his mouth with his hand. Laurel seemed grotesque to him. This posing was someone else's idea of sex, not his. The small, subtle things about women turned him on: the arc of a neck, the slant of a leg, the forgiving grace of a smile.

"Why don't you try posing?" Laurel asked. "C'mon. It'll be fun. Like kids playacting."

Laurel pulled Dan up by the arm so that he was standing in front of her on the kitchen linoleum. He tried to sit down again.

"You're no fun," she said in a taunting schoolyard voice.

Under ordinary circumstances, Dan would take this as his cue to leave, but he'd had too much to drink, his brother was still missing. And here was his brother's inebriated wife; she was missing too. It was as if she'd slipped out of her body and into a cruel skin that had everything to do with Wake's absence. Dan should have warned Laurel years ago that Wake would do something like this, that he might disappear, but no one's ever that honest.

Dan was no longer here for support. He was here to reluctantly play a role, and the longer he played along, the more she might be freed of the rage she'd been repressing. It was his duty to sing when she said sing, to stand when she said stand, so he stood up and asked, "What do you want from me?" He stood there feeling her tight grip on his arm. For the first time that night, he felt how strong she really was, like some kind of bully, the kind who wasn't satisfied until somebody lost blood.

"Why don't you loosen up? Look at you. Khakis and an oxford." She bit her lip. A lock of hair fell over her face. "Take this off." She began to unbutton his shirt.

He grabbed her hands and held them at his chest, wanting to squeeze them hard, till it hurt, but held them gingerly instead, and she kept on unbuttoning. Laurel was grieving, he thought. She'd been abandoned and probably hadn't touched a man these last three months, and here she was putting her hands all over him.

Laurel was working on the third button, saying, "Get this shirt off. Just play along for a minute."

Dan gripped Laurel's cold hands in his. He'd neglected every brotherly duty in his life, including comforting Wake's wife. "Just for a minute," he said, releasing her hands.

It made him queasy to unbutton his shirt and hang it over the chair. He straightened the T-shirt he was wearing underneath and thought of how soon this would be over, how he could play along until he felt sober enough to drive home.

Laurel was inspecting him. "I think we should get out the camera. Take some pictures. Let's show Wake that he's not the only one having fun."

Laurel turned around and opened a kitchen drawer. "Look what I have," she said, wagging a disposable camera at Dan. "I bought it for Miles, but we can use it instead."

She held the camera up to her eye. The lighting in the kitchen was harsh, for working with knives, not cameras. Outside, no daylight remained.

"This isn't going to work," she said. "You aren't relaxed enough. Take off that T-shirt."

"Let's stop this." His hands were in fists.

"C'mon, Dan, take your T-shirt off. It's not like I've never seen a bare chest before." She put the camera on the table, stood up, and then her hands were on him, sweeping the crew neck over his chin and nose. Her breath stank of bourbon.

"That's enough," he protested, but Laurel wouldn't stop.

"Let's get you posed," she said. Then her fingers jabbed him as she straightened his lower back and flattened his stomach, every touch rough and loveless. He thought of the doctor who'd been feeling around his testicles in a way that made him nervous, how his body went rigid, how he wanted to stand on his toes and tighten the tendons in his feet when the doctor squeezed and said, "This here. Yes, here. A lump."

"Look at you," Laurel said. "Can't you try to be just a little bit sexy? It's sad, really, how some people just don't have it." She cupped both of her hands over his bare chest where his breasts would be if he were a woman. "No curves. No bounce. But you'll have to do."

She moved back to her director's chair and sat with her toes curled around the edge of the canvas seat. Camera poised, she said, "Ready?"

When the flash went off, she let out a laugh that cut him.

"Your pants. Off with your pants," she demanded, viewing him through the camera. "Off with your pants, I say!"

"Don't." His voice was feeble. That day at the doctor's office, while the doctor went out to get a second opinion, Dan stood there with nothing but a paper gown on. He looked out the window onto bungalows with flat rooftops covered in rain puddles. He'd later go to one of those bungalows to get his radiation therapy. In the distance, small and far off, was the Arch and downtown Saint Louis where he worked. From the other side of the hospital, he would have been able to see the green sea of treetops near his home. There he was, stuck somewhere in the middle—not at work, not at home, neither. The next thing he knew, two doctors entered the room, and he had to open his gown while a new doctor examined his testicles, pressing, squeezing for the lump. Dan kept looking out that window, thinking how all he wanted was one little pill, just one little pill to make it all go away.

"Let's see what you're all about," Laurel said. "Off with it."

Dan waited for Laurel's tone to soften, to end this charade, but her voice was slippery with alcohol. Embarrassment spread over his skin. He felt peeled back, exposed, imperfect. It had not been that long ago, only six months, since the day he'd had the bandages removed from where his testicle had been, and he stood before the bedroom mirror, looking at himself. "It's not noticeable," Irene assured him. "From certain angles, maybe, yes . . . but I'm the only one who'll know."

"C'mon, Dan. Stop being such a woman," Laurel said with the camera over her eye.

Dan moved his hands from his sides and touched his belt buckle, though he hadn't meant to touch it. The camera flash went off and struck him again and again, a frenzy of light. He put up a hand to shield his eyes. The shutter released. The film advanced. More blinding light struck him. He staggered forward, weakened, and put his palm out to brace himself against the table. He couldn't move. Half naked, he felt trapped here in this house, trapped here in this kitchen.

9

"Oh, boo!" Laurel said when it was all over. "You didn't reveal a thing!"

Laurel put the camera down and dribbled a little more bourbon into her glass. She'd had too much to drink but wanted to keep the unbalanced feeling going. Then she thought of Wake, and her mood was ruined. She drained the dark-caramel liquid from the bottom of her glass. "I can't help but feel that Wakefield is out there in the wilderness," she began, "and if he knew what was happening, he'd be laughing at us—how we're all shut up indoors, drinking his bourbon, reading his magazine."

Dan turned away and saw his image caught in the reflection of the window over the kitchen sink, bare-chested and pale, looking sick. He thought about his testicle, his own flesh cut off from him, gone.

It had been a mistake, this distance, this lost brother who never knew about the cancer. The radiation therapy took only a month, and in that month, not a single phone call from his brother came. Three months passed, then six, then Wake was gone, and, no, he was never coming back. A three-month vanishing act was a lifetime compared to three days.

"I have to leave," Dan said, reaching for his T-shirt. He quickly slipped it on and put his business shirt over it, then buttoned his shirt while walking to the front door. "I have housework to get done."

"Wait." Laurel followed him to the door. She didn't know what to say. His sudden leaving triggered a feeling of dread, and she was too wobbly with bourbon to get the right words out. "Don't leave."

Dan exhaled through his nose. "I've had enough," he said. The words felt hard in his mouth, the way honesty sometimes feels like brutality.

He turned and opened the door, ready to walk through the storm. The air between them was mossy and wet.

"You can't go," she said.

"What more could you possibly want?"

She wanted to tell him the truth: that she wasn't fine, that she wasn't strong, that it was all an act.

"Listen," she said, realizing that she hadn't brought up the subject of geishas. "Wait." But he was already stepping into the rain and heading for the SUV's door.

10

A few weeks after Dan's wife had picked up Miles, Laurel developed the film in her disposable camera. She wanted to see something that would make her feel good, images of Miles playing with blocks on the floor. Instead she saw Dan standing in her kitchen with his shirt off. She'd expected the photos to be comical, a parody of domestic sexuality. But the lighting captured the creases around his mouth, the awful contortion of his face. The pictures conjured the image of that abandoned wife in Victorian England. Laurel imagined that woman crawling into bed at night with a kerchief to her lips, lying there in private agony, then rising the next morning to put on her dress and pin her hair into a bun. She imagined how the woman checked her naked face in the mirror each day, how she practiced the smile that looked the least bitter, how every rehearsed moment concealed her heartache. That production went on as long as her husband was gone. For twenty years, 7,300 consecutive days. The dress. The hair. The smiles. Then Laurel thought of herself: she was only ninety-nine days in.

IRON

"I need an iron," he said to the bartender, as he raised his rumpled suit sleeve. "You'd think the hotels in this town would have irons. But no! No irons. No laundry service. Nothing." He nursed a Heineken, then turned to the woman sitting beside him. She was thirty-something and slightly overweight. Her curly brown hair was held back with a banana clip. He explained that he'd have to deliver a sociology lecture the next morning in a wrinkled suit.

She smiled, then said, "I have an iron."

Thirty minutes later, they'd left the bar and entered the hallway of her apartment building. Someone had recently moved out. A misshapen cardboard box littered the hallway floor along with a stray playing card—the Jack of Clubs. They passed an apartment with a brick propping open its door; inside the vacant unit, playing cards were strewn about.

"What a mess," she said, her eyes shy, cast downward. She inserted her key into her door's lock. "College towns . . . you know how they are."

"Yeah . . . well . . . I guess nobody stays in one place for long," he said.

"Well . . . nobody stays." She opened the door. "And nobody really cares about the mess they leave behind."

He stood at the threshold of her apartment and caught a whiff of burnt toast. It was a one-bedroom unit with a futon. She walked him through a kitchen that served as a corridor to the bedroom.

"Go ahead and undress," she said as she led him to a pink-tiled bathroom.

He shut the bathroom door behind him and scanned a tray of face creams and lipsticks until he found a tube of Colgate toothpaste, then quickly finger-brushed his teeth. He felt giddy and uncertain about this woman. Outside, he heard her open an ironing board's squeaky legs. He waited for her to offer him a drink—beer, wine. She offered nothing.

He undressed down to his boxers. Stupidly, he hadn't worn a T-shirt beneath his business shirt. Now in the mirror, he saw a slob: hairy-nippled, slightly overweight, and about to iron the same suit he'd worn earlier on the plane. "Should I come out?" he asked through the door. "I'm only wearing socks and boxers," he explained.

She laughed. "Come on out. I've seen plenty of undressed men before."

He walked through the kitchen with his suit cradled against his bare chest. "I can iron it myself," he said.

"Allow me," she replied as she gathered up his clothes.

He took a seat on the edge of the futon, conscious of his seminudity. "You really don't have to iron it."

"I want to." Her eyes met his with warmth. "I like to iron."

When she began to press his lapels, he was reminded of an image from a 1950s *Good Housekeeping* ad he often used for an Intro to Sociology assignment. The ad was the stylized image of a beautiful housewife in a crisp yellow dress with a cinched waist, a woman divorced from her sexuality, head lowered in servitude, ironing. It was not the image of the woman in front of him now; this woman in jeans and a loose black tank top was not pretty or proper. Beauty was distant and cruel, he now realized, like a weapon. And here was this unbeautiful woman . . . defenseless. Yet graceful. She ironed with a sensitivity to every crease. Beauty in servitude, he thought.

His own wife, before she left, never ironed for him, not once. They'd rarely done favors for each other. If his wife were here now, she'd make him stand naked over the hot iron, and she'd make sure he worked hard to straighten things out.

"You live alone?" he asked.

"Isn't it obvious?" The iron hissed with steam as she flattened his slacks on the board. "Well," she said. "I haven't always lived alone."

Embarrassed, he hugged a pillow over his boxers. The apartment seemed orderly and vacant. No pizza boxes. No empty wine bottles.

She looked up from her ironing, and he hugged the pillow tighter.

"Relax," she said, gliding the iron up to the inseam of his slacks. "Plenty of men have seen me naked."

"Did any of them iron your suits?" he asked.

She thought for a second, then said, "No."

For some peculiar reason he liked this: He liked watching this woman; he liked the whole idea of it, knowing that she wanted to work for him, that she liked this kind of servitude. He wanted to stay forever in this moment and be served.

"You don't like messes," he observed. "I mean, you seem like a very clean person."

"I guess I like clean living," she said.

When she finished, she handed him his slacks, and he put the suit on in front of her, first one leg, then the other, a striptease in reverse. The fabric was warm against his skin. When he began to put on the shirt, her eyes watched every button pass through every eyelet. He made a show of dressing the way a newlywed might exaggerate and flirt, except he coyly let everything that was once intimate and vulnerable fasten shut. Finally he got around to his necktie, and she stopped him.

"I'll tie it," she said.

She moved him against the ironing board so she could work under the light. Her crabbed fingers gripped the tie. He waited for their eyes to meet, so she would see that she had him.

She smiled, pleased, but didn't look up. "Wouldn't it be nice if women and men could always get along like this?" she asked as she looped the bottom of the tie down through the knothole. "Wouldn't it be nice if men and women could do favors for each other and never expect anything in return?" She was still smiling that downcast smile, her eyes concentrating on the craftsmanship of tying a knot.

His heartbeat became reckless, and he took a deep breath. Somewhere behind him, the cooling iron ticked.

"Yes. That would be nice," he replied, not overthinking it, not ruining the moment with the truth.

THE LAST PERFECT DAY

1

Joey was thirteen and had recently discovered he could sweat. The mist of perspiration that he used to call sweat hadn't really been sweat at all. This new sweat dripped down his temples like blood and made him feel like the world was sucking out his insides one drop at a time. That's what it felt like: all the sweat and exhaust fumes and honking horns of rush hour in Hollywood. The world was burning him up.

Joey and his friend Derrick walked home from band practice down Las Palmas Avenue, off the main drags of Santa Monica and Highland where traffic amplified the heat. Flat-faced apartment buildings lined the block, all of them three stories high and pastel green, blue, or orange. Open windows, where fans listed hazardously, expelled the indoor heat. On one ledge a pot of azaleas wilted in the sun. Further down a pink bath rug hung from a window like an unfurled tongue.

"You thirsty?" Derrick asked and pushed his glasses up his nose.

"We shoulda stopped for a Big Gulp," Joey replied.

At the end of the block they came upon a green garden hose on the sidewalk. The foam of a freshly washed car trickled down the gutter.

"Thank God," Derrick said, dropping his clarinet case and book bag to the ground. He followed the hose through some oleander bushes.

Joey let his backpack drop to the curb. When the hose sprang to life, water hit the pavement and steamed. The metal nozzle thwacked against the sidewalk, and a rainy smell filled the air. Joey grabbed the neck of the hose and savored the warm metallic water, spraying the water over his face, letting it run into his mouth.

"Gimme some," Derrick said as he came out from the oleander bushes.

Joey wiped his mouth with the back of his hand and gave Derrick the hose. Derrick put his glasses in his shirt pocket, then wiggled a spray of water onto his sun-pinked forehead. Across the street, Joey looked up at a blue stucco apartment building and saw a baby's pale face peering out from an open window on the second floor. The fuzzy head bobbed. Fat little arms held its chest up. A gummy pink smile spread across the baby's face. Joey looked into the other windows, seeing hanging ferns, a bird cage, and shut drapes. His eyes went back to the baby as it reached out over the ledge, then gripped the curtain. Its black eyes blinked in the sunlight.

While Derrick hosed the heat off his bare legs, sticking his thumb over the nozzle to get a cool spray, Joey stepped into the street. A chubby baby arm waved out at him, all the way out the window, flagging him down like a woman in distress.

"Hey," Joey yelled up at the window, squinting hard. "Hey, somebody! Your baby!"

Nothing. No response. The baby leaned forward and let out a wail. Gravel slid under Joey's feet as he sprinted toward the pink blur tumbling from the window.

2

"That's how it happened," he told his sister Mona. "Like slow motion. And I ran, and the baby fell in my arms."

"You're so full of crap," she interrupted.

Mona stood straight-backed in a black suede vest and studied herself in the mirror. She backed up to get a better look. Joey sat on the unmade bed behind her and hugged a pillow.

"It's true," Joey said. "Derrick saw it happen. The baby started screaming when it landed, and I didn't know what to do."

"And now you're a hero," she said to his mirror image.

"*No.* It was terrible. The baby didn't come fluttering down. It came down heavy. It happened so fast."

"But you just said it happened in slow motion."

"It's the truth!"

"Yeah . . . right." Mona cut her eyes at his reflection.

Joey didn't feel like talking about it anymore and waited for Mona to say something else. Mona picked up a brush and stroked her hair back. She was only seventeen and wiry white strands were already sprouting around her ears. Her brush snagged on a snarl.

"Shit! Are you gonna sit there all day?!" she asked the mirror. "I've got things to do, and you're reeking up my room. Go take a shower or put on some deodorant or something."

Joey pulled his shirt away from his chest and smelled it. "I don't have any deodorant."

"Go find some, Stoop."

Joey walked into the bathroom. His hands were covered with dried baby snot and tears. In the medicine cabinet, he rummaged around until he found a glass bottle of amber-colored cologne. He splashed some onto his hands then patted it under his arms. The cologne was the last relic left behind by Joey's father. Four years after his parents' separation, it still sat hidden behind a box of baking soda. The cologne was heavy and artificially sweet. To Joey, it smelled like guilt. A brown crust had congealed beneath the cap and around the rim of the bottle. Joey couldn't remember smelling the scent on his father. It was Joey's own sweat that reminded him of the sharp aroma when his father came home from a dig in Death Valley with yellow stains under his arms and a canvas bag full of dusty excavation gear at his side.

Joey hadn't seen his father for six months, not since he'd flown to L.A. for a paleontology convention. They had only one Saturday afternoon together before his father went back to Wyoming. Most of the afternoon was spent roaming downtown L.A.'s stark concrete streets and looking up at the 1920s art deco and Beaux-Arts buildings around the hotel. Few cars or people were on the sidewalks. The low roar of the freeway droned between the buildings. Late in the afternoon, they drove to the busier streets of Hollywood and had an impromptu picnic on the landscaped lawns of the La Brea Tar Pits.

They were sitting on the grass at the La Brea Tar Pits when his father said, "This is how it is. Los Angeles . . . it's slowing down, gumming up. First there'll be water wars. Then heat extinction."

His father looked out at the cars on Wilshire Boulevard. Beyond the wrought-iron gates of the tar pits was a traffic jam. Crumbs fell onto his shaggy beard when he bit into his turkey sandwich. They sat in front of a fenced observation pit where a life-size reproduction of a mammoth was stuck in a lake of tar. The mammoth appeared to be struggling in the tar with her tusks upraised. Her trunk silently trumpeted to another mammoth that watched from the safety of the shore, under the shade of the palm trees by Wilshire Boulevard.

"How long until humans go extinct?" Joey asked.

"It depends. Animal extinction occurs when the environment becomes uninhabitable, when there's a harsh climatic change, habitat destruction, excessive predation . . . but humans can adapt to hostile environments." He threw the remaining crust of his sandwich to the sparrows and pigeons scavenging in the grass. "What's important is that the environment might become too hostile for animals or plants to survive. A single broken link in our symbiotic relationship with nature can wipe out the human race. For instance, if ants go extinct, then there'll be nothing to aerate the soil, and humans will die of starvation."

"But how long?" Joey asked. "How many years till *humans* go extinct?"

"Thousands of years from now or maybe the next several centuries. Who knows? It only takes one broken link. If that broken link exists, then we might already be dead."

Joey sunk his fingers into the grass. "Isn't there anything we can do?"

"The whole world has to change, Joey. You can't change anything alone."

All his academic life Joey had read books where a few men changed the course of history. He couldn't understand what made *that* world so different from *this* world.

"Maybe we need to start a revolution," Joey said.

His father laughed so loud that he scared away the pigeons. "So you want to be an eco-terrorist when you grow up? Spiking trees? Those people do more harm than good. They hurt a lot of people."

"But don't people get hurt in revolutions? Wouldn't that be better than human extinction?"

His father was still laughing, but Joey didn't think there was anything funny about it.

"Who are you going to kill? Every person that doesn't get a water-conservation toilet?"

"I don't want to kill anyone. Never mind. I don't want to talk about this anymore."

Joey looked toward the glossy layer of water that covered the tar pit. The water had deceived numerous animals, luring them into the tar. Underneath, crude oil and asphaltum seeped up from the earth. Violet-blue pools of oil bled into the black lacquer of water.

"Don't worry," his father said. "You'll be dead long before humans go extinct."

"Dad . . . I *know* that."

The grass made Joey's legs itch. He was annoyed but didn't complain. He never spent enough time with his father to complain. Still, he didn't want to go to the Tar Pits. He didn't want to look up at buildings. He didn't want to eat sandwiches. He wanted to sit down with his father, face-to-face, at a decent restaurant. He wanted to talk with his father about life, not death.

"Okay. Okay. New topic," his father replied. "You know this dig I'm working on? Well, kids come by the site all the time on their dirt bikes, asking about what we've found. But those kids are only interested in the theatrical stuff like T. Rex fossils and pterodactyls. They don't give a damn about the little stuff like the chondricthyans or the osteichthyans."

Beyond his father, Joey watched a procession of elementary school kids walk hand-in-hand, a human chain, yammering and laughing and guiding each other out of the park.

"Hey listen," his father said and started fishing through the pocket of his blue jeans. The jeans were more brown than blue, and the knees were worn down to strings. Joey noticed the age spots on his father's face. Wrinkles branched down his cheeks like the shattered surface of a desert basin. Ravines formed at the corners of his eyes when he squinted. His father dug the heels of his beat-up cowboy boots into the grass. He finally produced what he was looking for. "Here," he said. "It's the tooth of a thecodont from the Triassic period, very rare, an ancestor of the lizard."

In the callused palm of his hand was a tiny fang. Joey put it in his pocket. His father always brought a memento, usually a fragment of broken bone. Joey had a shoe box crammed under his bed full of crumbling toe bones and chipped teeth from animals whose names he could no longer remember.

"Next time I'll bring you the vertebra of an ectotherm," he said.

Joey nodded and stared out at the mired mammoth.

3

The night the baby fell, Joey stayed up late. He stretched out on the couch and read a science fiction novel that he'd rescued from the street. He'd found it with its pages spread open and flattened against the pavement. The spine of the book was cracked, and each page was wavy and warped from sitting too long in the sun. Some pages were chewed up from being run over by cars. It wouldn't stay closed unless he put his mother's marble ashtray on the cover to keep the pages from fanning.

When he first noticed the book, he was attracted by the shimmering picture of Earth on the cover. It was titled *The Last Perfect Day*. He liked the way the title sounded. That's why he picked the book up and dusted off the grainy pebbles embedded in the pages. He wanted to read about *any* perfect utopian day. To his disappointment, the novel was about the last five days before the apocalyptic crash of a giant comet.

When he heard his mother's keys at the front door, he placed the book on his chest.

"What are you doing up at this Nowhere Hour?" his mother asked after she came in.

The *Nowhere* Hour used to be the *Know Where* Hour, a time when Joey "knew where he should be," which was in bed. Ever since his mother had gone back to school for her chemistry PhD, he'd translated it to the Nowhere Hour.

Joey looked up at his mother's silhouette in the doorway. The frame of her skirt made a triangle. Her shoes were flat and wide. He could smell the latex from the lab gloves she'd been wearing.

"I wanted to tell you something," he said.

She went into the bathroom. He heard her unzip her skirt. "I don't have much time. That lab report is due tomorrow," she said through the crack of the bathroom door. "What's so important?"

"I don't know," he replied. "Nothing, I guess."

Joey went to bed stifling a crushed feeling in his chest, like his soul was crumpled up in his ribcage. The image of the falling baby looped in his brain. When the baby landed in his arms, Joey brought it toward his chest and sunk his fingers into its plump stomach and legs. Screams shivered against his hands. Its face turned red and wrinkled up. Joey felt the baby's heart hammering. At first, he wanted to put that baby down on the curb and run away.

Derrick watched the whole thing from across the street with the hose swinging from his hand. "I don't believe it. I don't believe it," he exclaimed as water gushed over the sidewalk.

4

The next morning, Joey woke up feeling like there was a magnet in his stomach pulling him down. On the walk to school, he took a different street than usual and went straight to the bungalow where his homeroom was. While he was waiting outside for the bell to ring, he watched the laundry service on the other side of the gate. Bundles of grayed laundry bags shimmied on industrial conveyor lines two stories up. They circled in and out of the portals between two buildings. Five days a week he looked up and saw those bags. He never thought about it until that moment, but he was small enough to fit in one of those bags. In fact, he wasn't entirely sure that those bags were full of laundry. They might be full of cement. Just last week Joey played a sack of cement in a Human Relations class dramatization.

While he was still looking up someone touched his hand and asked, "Is it true?"

"What?" He turned and saw Lynn Smithe.

"Somebody heard you caught a baby."

Joey shook his head. "It was nothing. It just happened."

"But it's true. It really happened." She turned around and waved over Janice and the six-foot-tall stoner named Yakov. "It's true! Come over here."

They circled around Joey, and he told the story of how the baby fell into his arms. "No big deal," he said.

"Joe-Joe is the *maaan*," Yakov said. He gave Joey's shoulder a squeeze. "Can't you just imagine all the brains on the sidewalk if you hadn't caught it?" Yakov put his hand in the air and lowered it to the whistling noise of a bomb dropping.

Lynn grimaced. "That baby was lucky."

"Yeah," Yakov replied. "It could have slipped right through his fingers. Whoops . . . splat!"

For the rest of the day, kids congratulated Joey and clapped him on the back. "Tell us how it happened," they asked. "What did it look like when it was falling down?"

During band practice, Joey came up behind Derrick while he was putting his clarinet together. Students warmed up on their instruments. Flutes played scales. A trumpet announced a horse race.

"What'd you go and tell everyone for?" Joey asked over the din of instruments.

Derrick took the reed he was moistening out of his mouth. "I thought you'd want people to know."

"I don't even want to talk about it."

"What's wrong?" Derrick's eyes narrowed behind his glasses. "You did a good thing."

"But I didn't do anything."

The band teacher rapped his baton against the podium. Tap tap tap. And there was silence.

5

The baby had just started bawling in Joey's arms when Derrick turned off the hose and ran to his side.

"Take it," Joey said. Holding the baby under its arms, he pushed it toward Derrick.

"No, you keep it."

"But I don't want it." Joey squinted up at the window and expected someone to look out.

Derrick ran into the street and cupped his hand around his mouth. "Is anybody up there?"

There was no response. The baby's crying grew louder.

"I'll go up and knock on some doors," Derrick said. He ran to the front door of the apartment building. It was locked.

"C'mon, Derrick. Hurry!"

"Stay here," Derrick said. "I'll go home and get my grandmother. She'll know what to do."

"Just hurry," Joey replied. He couldn't stand the noise of the baby, so he shifted the baby's position and held it like a mother would, cradled on its back.

"I'll be right back," Derrick said. "I promise."

Derrick picked up his book bag and clarinet case. He left Joey standing in the sun, clumsily holding the baby in his arms. Joey couldn't get a grip on the bulky diaper. The baby hadn't stopped crying, and Joey feared he might hurt it if he moved the wrong way. A few cars whizzed by. Down the street, a man got into a car and drove off. Joey was sweating like crazy now. His shirt was stuck to his back. Perspiration ran down his chest. The baby seemed heavier and heavier, and the cries sounded more demanding.

"Shhh," he said. "Stop that. Shh."

Joey felt like crying too. Something drizzled down his face. It could have been sweat or tears, he didn't know which. He licked his salty lips and looked for a place to sit. The entrance to the apartment building was set in from the sidewalk. Pale blue paint covered a slab of cement by the door. It was the only shaded place to sit, so he knelt down against the wall next to a plastic-grass welcome mat. A line of ants rose out of a jagged crack in the cement and trailed into some white landscaping rocks beside the building. Joey thought about how much easier it would be if he could find a cool spot on those white rocks and put the baby down. He could look the other way and ditch the baby in some underbrush. But it was a living, breathing human—a huge responsibility.

The baby began to calm down. Its breathing eased when Joey gently rocked from side to side. A swirl of downy black hair and long eyelashes made Joey think it was a girl. He'd never seen anything as extraordinary as her runny red nose and fingers; even her fingernails were amazing. She looked up at him and expressed relief with her eyes. They stared at each other, and she smiled when he smiled. Her tiny fingers clasped his shirt. She made talking noises.

"Yes," he whispered. "I won't leave."

She giggled when he tickled her chin but scrunched up her nose when he cleaned her face with his shirt hem. When Joey scrunched up his nose, she smiled at him. It was a little game. She laughed at every face he made, even when he made a pouty sad face and stuck out his lip.

When he heard someone walking toward him, Joey looked up. A girl in yellow shorts with tan legs stopped to remove the foil from a pack of cigarettes. Her expression changed when she saw the baby.

"What's going on?!" she demanded and charged toward Joey. "How did you get my baby?"

"Wait!" Joey stood up and drew the baby toward him. "Wait a minute!"

She snatched the baby from Joey so fast that he was left cradling air. The baby started screaming.

"I'm calling the cops," the girl said. She fumbled with her key in the lock of the door and dropped her cigarettes on the welcome mat.

"You better not have hurt her," she said once she'd gotten the door open, checking her crying baby's face.

Joey said nothing. The baby kept wailing. Wails rang in his ears even after he watched her turn and take the baby away.

Across the street, Joey's backpack sat on the curb beside the hose. He slung the backpack over his shoulders and saw Derrick round the corner, guiding his grandmother by the arm. She appeared to have just awakened from either a nap or the hypnotic trance of TV. Her hair was disheveled. Clownish purple slippers covered her feet. She slipped a bony hand into the pocket of her apron and pulled out rumpled tissue to dab her forehead. Embroidered onto her apron was a goose wearing a bonnet.

"What happened?" Derrick asked. "Where'd the baby go?"

Joey shook his head. "What's it matter?" he said, not wanting to explain. "None of it makes any sense."

Alone, walking home, he couldn't get the baby out of his mind. She was right there in his arms, this beautiful human life. He could still smell her on his hands, and yet he couldn't help but see her thousands of years from now, beneath the weight of the world, just a few hairs and some fragments of bone. No scientist would save her from heat extinction. No archaeologist would preserve her brittle bones.

HONEYMOON IN BEIRUT

1

In 1975, during the autumn of the Defense Industry, the Golden Age before Hughes Aircraft fell to General Motors, a Lebanese dressmaker by the name of Emile Saleem Haddad fell in love with a bolt of fabric. This happened in the City of Angels, where each Saturday before dawn a lively fashion bazaar spilled onto the streets of the Garment District. Merchants pushed dress racks out to the loading zones and draped gabardine slacks over cardboard drums. Inside the warehouses, shoppers mulled around towering bolts of textiles, a Parthenon of purple velvet pillars and toppled camelhair columns. In this wondrous place, this City of Angora and Acrylic, Emile lost his head over fine Oriental silk.

It was love, his wife Zahlah knew. Though married only nine months, she could see that Emile had gotten the lint in his eyes and could no longer see straight. Before their marriage, Emile was seduced by fine black wool that was heavy and soft, wool sweetly spiced with incense like an old widow's church clothes. Hundreds of *lira* were spent to design a spectacular coat with large custom glass buttons the size of *piasters*. Under each button, Emile placed an ancient photograph of a woman's face. Gold filigree clasps held down these photos of serious spook-eyed women, strange and unsmiling, the cutouts from wedding portraits depicting conjugal gloom—all of them the wives of arranged marriages. When Emile first presented the coat to Zahlah, cradling it with trembling pride, she received it with a sense of wonderment at its beauty, not recognizing those distant, unfamiliar faces in the buttons. These women were Zahlah's great-aunts and great-grandmothers, Emile explained to her, images he'd pleaded for late one night after Zahlah's mother had loosed her hair from its chignon, letting it fall long and dark over her nightdress. Zahlah could practically see the grimace on her mother's face as she knifed the yellowed photographs from the insides of lockets like the flesh from the shell of an oyster. Such destruction for a few photographs, such emotional expense.

The day Emile presented Zahlah with the coat, he'd said, "When we reach the American Promised Land, you will never be alone. See? You will have your whole family on your sleeve." When she arrived in California, however, Zahlah had no need for an overcoat. It never rained, never snowed, never even got cold in Los Angeles, so her ancestral coat remained boxed with mothballs in the bedroom closet, forgotten like the women knifed out of old lockets.

As they drove away from the Los Angeles Garment District that Saturday morning in 1975, Zahlah stared at the back of her husband's head. He and his friend Marouf sat in the front seat. She felt like a child sitting behind them. Only once did Emile swivel in his seat to look into the backseat at Zahlah and her brother Ramsey who'd moved to Los Angeles to finish medical school. The bolt of silk sat between Zahlah and Ramsey, propped upright like a silly giraffe. Emile then told Zahlah they would have to be more frugal for a while. "We'll have to eat *mujadarra* instead of meat," he said. "And there will be no honeymoon in Beirut. Not this summer. Not even this winter."

Zahlah tightened her kerchief around her chin and didn't reply. When they moved to the United States, Emile told her that America would be their honeymoon, an eternity of California sunshine, but she demanded a real honeymoon, a return home where they could stay at a Mediterranean resort.

Marouf raised his bushy eyebrows at her in the rearview mirror. "Don't worry, Zahlah. Beirut will be there next year."

"But mother has been writing of civil unrest," she said. "Just last month, a Palestinian taxi driver was pulled from his car and killed in the streets."

"Things will get better," Emile assured her. "Such fighting cannot last."

"Can't it?" her brother Ramsey interrupted. He leaned forward so he could be heard. "Beirut has already been destroyed and rebuilt six times. What difference would a seventh time make?"

Zahlah remained silent. Since their move to the United States, fighting continued to break out in the streets of Beirut. Barricades had been put up in their old neighborhood. Garbage was not being collected. Zahlah's mother wrote her to say that mortar shots regularly rattled her apartment windows in Ashrafiyeh.

"Next year Beirut. This year Los Angeles," Emile said.

"Next year is so far off." Zahlah sat back. Her fingers clutched the scarf under her chin.

"And not long from now," Ramsey interjected, "mother and *sitta* will have received their emigration papers to live with us in America."

"Next year is not so far off. You'll see," Emile said. Then there it was—the touch; Emile gave Zahlah's hand a light pat, one of his moments of strategic affection—a kiss to quell a complaint, an embrace to upturn a frowned face.

Later that evening, after dinner, Emile touched Zahlah again—twice in one day!—and almost as intimately as he'd touched her on their wedding night. "With your permission," he now said and held out the yellow measuring tape.

She delightedly breathed in his musky hair pomade as he took her measurements. Around her waist. Over her hips. So close to touching her, yet not really touching, never once stepping out of professional decorum to have a moment of play with his wife—a pinch of her behind, a lingering hand on her hip. Instead he wound the tape behind her back and pulled it taut into a thin hug across her breasts.

"Why does it feel like you are measuring my body for a coffin?" she asked.

"Hush," he said, loosening the tape.

"Did you know ten people died in a mortar attack in Beirut yesterday?"

"I read it in *Al-Safir*."

"Did you know Abu Saleem, the coffin maker? He died in a recent bombing in Ashrafiyeh."

"Zahlah, quiet!" Emile said as he knelt to measure her waist.

Zahlah looked down at his sleek hair. "I remember Abu Saleem coming to our apartment when my father died. He came with his pet dog, a little terrier that lapped some spilled milk off the kitchen floor."

Emile let out a breath through his nose.

"He had webbed feet," she said.

Emile put down his measuring tape and looked up at her. "The dog?"

"No. The coffin maker. The coffin maker had webbed feet."

"Let me work," he said, then placed the tape measure around her hips.

When Zahlah introduced her family to Emile, when he sat in her mother's front room and sipped tea from a china cup, Zahlah wondered if even then he'd been thinking she'd make a good clothes rack. Her shy hips and long legs were ideal for modeling garments. She was taller than he by an inch, and Emile never mentioned it, not once.

The first time Emile met her mother and *sitta*, her grandmother, Emile spoke softly of his childhood in the hill country, where he and Marouf had grown up. Both moved to the city to attend the American University of Beirut. Emile studied art. Marouf studied engineering. It was only after Marouf took a ballistics engineering job in Los Angeles, designing bombs, that Emile began looking for a wife.

"Better to marry a dressmaker than a bomb maker," Zahlah's eighty-year-old *sitta* had interjected, crossing a traditional line of polite discourse and brazenly standing on the other side. There she was, a shrunken widow in black lacework, challenging Emile to cross the line with her. Such politics were not discussed publicly or privately, and Emile, in no position to silence her, listened to her prate about the Six-Day War of 1967, about how much she hated the Palestinian refugees who flooded into Beirut after the war, how she hated their dirty shanty towns.

"They wouldn't be so dirty if we helped them," Zahlah interrupted.

Zahlah's mother discreetly raised her eyebrows and continued to sip from her tea cup, saying nothing. *Sitta*, staring silently at her granddaughter, slowly freed her right arm from her lace shawl.

"And why," *sitta* asked, "why should we help them? Why ... when they don't belong here in the first place?" She spoke in a falsetto and punctuated every thought with a subtle hand gesture, an "O" formed by pinching her index finger to her thumb; between those pinched fingers she gently tugged an invisible thread. "The Palestinians—they are an eyesore with their slums and barefoot children selling flowers on the street," she said, tugging the thread. "It's a good thing the government built a high wall around their slum in Qarantina to hide them." She tugged twice, tightening a knot of silence.

Zahlah bit her tongue to conceal her irritation. She taught French at the *Dekwaneh* refugee camp for Christian

Palestinians. These were people who had lost their homes and the ancestral property that had been in their families for centuries. Now they were displaced, homeless, forced to scatter among unsanitary dwellings with no home to return to.

Emile had been sitting there meekly, too shy to even glance Zahlah's way. Finally he sat up to straddle the line that divided polite and impolite discourse, saying, "Do you not think the walls of Qarantina are an oversimplified solution to a complex problem?"

"Walls or no walls," *sitta* retorted. "It's the Palestinians that remain the problem."

Emile merely gave a light shrug.

Zahlah could no longer remain silent and said, "Walls only cover up what the government does not want us to see, so we can pretend it's not there and go on with our lives. Those walls are the biggest problem of all."

At that, Zahlah's mother released a breathy laugh. "Enough . . . enough . . . perhaps you would like some more tea? Yes? Good!" she said, nodding. "More tea for everyone. Come help me with the tea," she said to Zahlah.

In the kitchen, her mother, tight-lipped, stroked back the freed strands of hair that had strayed from her chignon.

"Well?" Zahlah asked her mother.

"He's well-mannered," her mother said, then turned to look Zahlah in the eye. "Manners are good," she replied, nodding firmly.

Zahlah nodded back, eyes jeweled with delight, and her heart burst into a bouquet of *Yeses. Yes,* she would be permitted to court Emile. *Yes,* she would marry him. *Yes,* she would *yes* by his side.

But in America Zahlah felt so much anxiety that everything Emile said or did made her heart shake out a silent *No.* Emile himself was full of *Nos.*

"Don't you want to measure my neck?" she asked when he finished her measurements for the silk dress.

"No."

She touched her throat. "Last time you needed my neck."

"Last time I made you a coat, not a dress."

Emile unrolled several yards from the top of the bolt in the gesture of spinning a ballerina.

"Look at how it sways and moves. See how kinetic it is? Its vitality?" He lay several yards of fabric over a chivalrous arm and moved it to and fro in a dance. "It moves like a movie star," he said. Releasing it gently, sliding it from his arm, he let the silk pool on the rug, where it shimmered and rippled as though some elegant American actress from the '30s had melted on the floor.

It was on the plane to the United States that Emile confessed his passion for American cinema, telling Zahlah of the movie house in Beirut that showed old American films, a small theater with cheap wooden seats that squeaked whenever the patrons crossed or uncrossed their legs. There was no screen, only a naked wall. This was in Southern Beirut, on the Rue Ahmed Chaoqui, away from the resorts and the honey-sweet smell of bakeries, amidst the scrabble of high-rise apartment buildings where kids yelled down from their balconies and chased each other through alleys. Old men in fez hats came in from playing *sija* and smoked cigars while they watched films in English, flickering and bright, with the light from the projector perforating the darkness to reveal billows of smoke. This was the dream of America that Emile ingested before emigrating, a dream tangled up in Ginger Rogers and Jean Harlow and the syrupy taste of port wine that old men passed from seat to seat. This was the dream, born of celluloid, made possible with silk.

2

"I think I have married an impotent man," Zahlah confessed one day. She was lounging under the backyard's lemon tree beside the empty pool. A jagged crack ran through the pool's bottom. Leaves had gathered around the drain. Rotting lemons, brown and moldering, lay down there in a smelly huddle.

Geta, Zahlah's only friend in Los Angeles, lived in the adjoining duplex. She had taken Zahlah under her wing, teaching her how to read a bus schedule and navigate the enormous California supermarkets. Geta sat up in her lounge chair, squinting as she reaffixed the safety pin that closed the deep V of her cleavage. Her broad shoulders had grown pink from the sun. "Impotent?" she asked in French. Neither she nor Zahlah spoke English. Geta was Basque but spoke fluent French and Spanish.

Beyond a slatted dividing fence, a man turned on his garden hose. Geta chinned toward him. "That journalist is looking at you again," Geta said in French, calling him a journalist because she'd seen him photograph a car accident on Los Feliz Drive. "Yes," she joked. "I think he's taking notes."

The journalist watched them from afar, smiled, and removed his hat to wave, revealing his yellowish bald head. Once, when Emile was not home, he hollered at Geta and Zahlah over the fence posts, saying, "You got nice lemons. Nice lemons." The women had shrugged, pretending to be confused, though they knew perfectly well what he'd said.

"Forget him," Zahlah said. "Listen to me. My husband would rather make a dress than touch his wife."

Geta brushed a fly from her leg. "You are an American woman now. Speak up! Tell him exactly what you want."

That night Zahlah watched Emile spread the fabric over his sewing table in their bedroom. He took his dress shears and gently cut the silk, lovingly pressing it down with his free hand, stroking it smooth. The fabric fell away from the blade without a frayed edge. It was a delicate operation, and he stayed in the room all night, cutting and clipping.

Zahlah lay in bed listening to his sewing machine yammer on and on like a nervous debutante. Periodically, she'd hear the anxious sound of scissors, slicing, a metallic whisper.

Already the bodice of the gown was done, and he had placed it on his dress dummy, raising the stand to its full height so that it towered over their tiny twin beds. In the old country, especially the hill country where Emile was from, couples did not sleep in the same bed; sometimes they didn't even sleep in the same room. And Emile was so modest that she'd never seen him in his undergarments. When he wanted to change clothes, he went into the bathroom. That night, after Emile crawled between his covers and turned out the nightstand light, Zahlah dangled an arm over the side of her bed and into the cold cavern of space between them.

"Emile," she said, "what kind of feelings do you have for me?"

"What are you talking about?"

She heard him turning in his bed, the tight crunching of stiff cotton sheets. The ghostly dress woman watched beyond their beds, a decapitated white blur. In the old country, her mother claimed to have seen a beheaded female ghost standing in front of the stove. Such headless ghost women were common, most wearing black mourning dresses and walking vacantly from room to room.

"What do you feel for me?" she asked.

"Shush," he replied.

"I have needs," she said. "Have you forgotten me?"

"Zahlah, go to sleep."

Not since their wedding night had they made love; when they were finally alone in a small hotel room with twin beds, Emile refused to touch her, so Zahlah offered herself to him, flattening her spine against the cold sheet. "I don't know what to do," he said as he began to make love. "It doesn't matter," she replied. "You will learn." Zahlah tried not to wince with pain as he clumsily forced himself into her—no beauty to the act, only necessity. Emile kept his eyes upward, never once daring to look down at her breasts. "I am so sorry, Zahlah, so sorry," Emile repeated. "Tell me to stop," he begged. "Please tell me to stop." Tears fell from the corners of her eyes, but she let him continue. A good wife, she didn't get angry or complain. When he finished, Emile made her sleep alone on the blood-anointed sheets. "Forgive me," he said, sliding into the comfort of his clean bed.

3

Was this wrong? This silk obsession? Something that she should be worried about? Zahlah didn't know. Weeks passed and she said nothing, letting him love the fabric, letting him show it off to the men who picked up their fitted Italian suits. Sometimes he trotted out the entire bolt, leaning it up against the closet door beside the TV, and he was doing something in his head when he looked at it, designing something, reupholstering his mental world in silk.

No dress deals had been cut, not with the Lebanese and Syrian businessmen who shook church incense from their clothes. No wedding dresses had been ordered from the silk swatch he carried in his breast pocket. It was the pearly luster. That was the problem. No one wanted a creamy off-white but only the whitest of whites for virgin brides. The last time Emile brought out the bolt, eager to entice a customer, his banter was filled with desperation, as if pleading to save his precious silk's life.

For weeks on end, there was no good news. Not even good mail arrived, just bills, until finally Zahlah received a letter from her mother. "The emigration papers have arrived," Zahlah told her brother Ramsey over the phone. "Mother and *sitta* found a cheap boat to America, *very* cheap!"

"How cheap?" her brother grumbled suspiciously.

"I don't know. Mother sold everything in the apartment at a great loss. They will dock in New York in six weeks."

"Well, I, too, have good news." Ramsey then announced that he'd been accepted to the cosmetic surgery residency at UCLA. A celebration was in order.

That afternoon Zahlah sat on a lounge chair by the sun-warmed concrete of the pool, rereading her mother's letter, when the bald journalist across the fence called out to her from where he'd been watering his bushes. He came over, producing a paper bag from his pocket, and pointed to the lemon tree.

"Lemons," he said, pointing to the tree again. His bald head gave off an oily shine.

Pocketing her letter, Zahlah yanked a half-dozen ripe lemons from the tree. Leaves rained onto her head. Rotten lemons thudded to the ground. She filled his paper bag, handing it back to him as he bowed to thank her. It was then that he motioned for her to follow him, guiding her to a gap at the corner of the fence, urging her with his voice to come.

The way he smiled at her, so open, so full of *Yes*—how could she spurn such an invitation? He was a harmless man, after all. She turned sideways to squeeze through the fence stakes. Short juniper bushes and trumpet-faced flowers bordered his house. His grass was soft with tender thin blades. The journalist opened a sliding glass door, leaving Zahlah on a brick patio. Moments later he returned with a large black camera, then gestured that he wanted to take her picture, that he wanted her to come out of the sunlight, pointing up at the brightness of the sky. "Come inside," he motioned.

Zahlah looked behind her, over the fence, searching for Geta or Emile. There was no one to stop her, no one to say, "No."

Inside, her bare feet stepped onto a plastic entry mat. She stood stiffly beside his TV set. A convertible couch with the bed out, sheets rumpled as if someone had just left, sat unabashedly in full view.

The journalist picked up a magazine with photos of women in fancy clothes. He pointed at each picture, saying something she didn't understand. Finally he stepped back and held up the camera, motioning that he wanted her to pose. He adjusted the lens over one eye, his fingers twittery with excitement. Zahlah, breathing deeply to settle herself, placed her arms at her sides. When the flash went off, adrenaline raced through her chest.

"Sit. Sit," he said, patting the unmade bed, repeating it until she reluctantly sat on the edge, her thighs cold against the aluminum frame, her pose rigid, like a mannequin, with her hands in her lap.

The journalist motioned for her to wait, then walked outside to pull a cluster of white pear blossoms from a tree in his yard. Returning, he presented her with the flowers, taking a tiny white blossom and tucking it behind her ear. He lingered with her hair, sinking his fingers between the strands, down to her naked scalp. Her hair, always tightly bound into a bun, he suddenly loosed, gently finding the pins, freeing her long black tresses so that they fell to the base of her spine.

His voice gushed with pleasure. *"Bella bella,"* he said, speaking in what she thought must be Italian, not French, though she understood what he meant.

Standing back, he took one photograph, then another, each from different angles. He touched her chin to position her face, his eyes meeting hers affectionately. Sitting there, she felt a knot of repression in her soul begin to slacken, freeing her enough to smile easily, playfully almost, smiles that warmed her entire face. There was something between them—between Zahlah and this man—a kind of spark or electricity that gave her a jolt whenever they made eye contact.

When the picture taking was over, he put his hand in hers to help her stand, sending a rush of giddiness to her head. Ugly as he was, she wanted to kiss him, to thank him, to give him something in return. Instead, she backed out the door and raced to her side of the fence where Geta was now standing at the mouth of the drained pool, hands firmly on her hips, wearing a loose bathrobe that revealed a long line of cleavage.

"What were you doing over there with the journalist?" Geta asked in a chastising voice as Zahlah slid between the fence posts.

"He showed me pictures. In a book," Zahlah replied in French.

"What type of pictures?"

"Pictures of women. Lots of women."

Geta's eyes lit up. "That man is in lust with you," she said. "Never go back. You hear me?"

4

Later that evening, Marouf and Ramsey came to dinner, and each brought bottles of anisette and wine. At the dining room table, Ramsey described the contrary logic of rhinoplasty, how you break a nose to set it straight.

"I could get rid of that bump." Ramsey tapped the bridge of his nose, looking at Zahlah sitting across from him. "I could give you a Marilyn Monroe nose. How would you like that?"

Zahlah pushed away from the table. "Stay away from my nose," she said jokingly before retreating into the kitchen where the oven timer had gone off. Ramsey continued talking at her through the open doorway.

"You see Marouf? I'm going to make him look like Clark Gable. I'm going to sculpt away that excess flesh."

Marouf, at the head of the table, had opened a second bottle of wine and began to pour some into his glass. Ramsey pushed up the septum of his own nose for Marouf to see what he'd look like.

"Why do you look at me like I'm an ugly foreigner?" she asked her brother when she brought the leg of lamb out on a carving board and set it on the table.

"Zahlah! I'm not looking at you like anything at all. I just want you to be more attractive."

"You are a butcher," she said, teasing him. "Now stop talking and carve the lamb."

Ramsey stood, raising his wineglass in the air. "Hey, Clark Gable," he said to Marouf. "Why don't you drag my brother-in-law from his sewing machine and bring him to the table?"

Marouf walked across the room, holding the neck of the wine bottle he'd opened and tapped its base against Emile's bedroom door. "It's time to eat, you madman."

Emile came out, the strain of sewing crimping his brow. "I'm no madman," he said as he sat beside his wife.

Ramsey carved the leg of lamb and placed slices of meat onto a serving platter.

"Look at that knife work," Marouf said. He spooned yogurt mint sauce onto his plate. "You are an artist, Ramsey."

"Emile is the one with the hands of a surgeon." Ramsey sat down. "Look at his long fingers. With all that practice hand-stitching, he could suture without leaving scars."

Emile grabbed his napkin and put both hands below the table. He lowered his head and shyly reached up to twinch his mustache. "Stop teasing me," he said.

"It's true. Look at my hands," Ramsey held up his palms. "Fat fingers. I'm lucky I don't cut someone's nose off. But you, Emile, you have the hands of an artist. And to think," he said, "your wife could be a work of art if only she let me fix that nose bump."

"Why not cut off my head?" Zahlah said. "Wouldn't that solve everything?"

"Zahlah!" Emile protested. "There's no harm in wanting you to look nice."

"But I'm *already* beautiful!"

Marouf suddenly stood up and teetered on one leg. "You want to see beauty? You want to see a work of art?" he asked. "I'll show you something more beautiful than an American blonde." Marouf walked out the front door, still wearing his napkin tucked into his belt.

Outside Marouf slammed the trunk of his Cadillac. He came back into the house holding an unremarkable sphere of metal the size of a lime with two aerodynamic vanes. "You see this? You will never see anything more beautiful than this in the world!"

"It's a piece of junk," Ramsey said.

"It's a bomb," he replied. "A cluster bomb that I designed—me!" He poked himself in the chest then gave the bomb a twist. Inside was a spiral chamber where all the tiny bomblets would be held. Marouf explained how the force of spinning would split each bomb open right before hitting the ground so that a sunburst of bomblets sprayed into the enemy.

He dropped the bomb into Zahlah's hands, and she prized it open to look at the spirals, like the inside of a halved snail shell.

"Something this simple and elegant," Marouf said. "*This* is beautiful."

"Why does beauty have to be so destructive?" Zahlah asked. She placed the bomb beside Marouf's wineglass.

Marouf sat down again. "What have you got to be so upset about, eh? All you need to do is sit around looking pretty."

Zahlah squeezed lemon onto her rice. "My brother and my husband say I'm not pretty enough."

"Well," Ramsey said, pushing his glasses up his nose. "Let's forget about this. The first thing I am going to do when *sitta* arrives is lop off those warty moles on her face."

Zahlah put her fork down. "Ramsey, stop it!"

"Stop it?" Ramsey asked. "Just a minute ago we were talking about bloody bombs."

"That's completely different," Marouf protested.

Ramsey cut apart the lamb on his plate. "Don't be so naïve," he replied. "Your bombs are for ethnic cleansing."

Zahlah threw her napkin on the table. "Bombs? Scalpels? What's the difference? Tell me!"

Zahlah looked to her husband, who'd been sitting there quietly sipping his anisette, his face innocent and blank as if lost in his world of silk. When she was about to say more, Emile reached under the table and held her hand, his warm sweet pulse in her palm, and he sat there, holding her curled fingers down in his lap without letting go. Emile then looked to the men and said something in English that Zahlah didn't understand, something that made them laugh.

Later that night, after everyone had left, Emile tippled one more glass of anisette before stumbling into the bathroom that adjoined their bedroom.

"Why didn't you defend me?" Zahlah asked him through the door while he changed clothes.

"From what?"

"From my brother who wants to cut off my nose. And from your best friend who threw a bomb at me. You should have intervened."

"What for? It was your battle, not mine."

Emile came out in his Woolworth's pajamas and got into bed. Zahlah unfastened her dress right in front of him, watching his face, his averted eyes, as she freed each button and let the dress drop. Underneath she was wearing a black slip. She let the slip drop too, the underclothes, everything.

"Turn out the light," Emile said, then rolled to his side with one hand over his eyes. "I don't want to argue."

"This isn't an argument." Zahlah left the light on and quickly pulled back her husband's covers.

"What's the matter with you?" he asked.

"I'm getting into bed with you."

She squirmed next to him and held her husband close, feeling the fuzziness of static electricity between them.

"Get into your bed," he hissed.

"*Biddi-yyaak*," she said softly. "I want you—inch by inch."

Emile lay there, rectilinear beneath the sheet. Zahlah slid her hand between the buttons of his shirt and touched the sweaty skin beneath the cotton, the hairs standing on end, the rough outline of his nipple.

"Tell me you want me," she said.

He said nothing, so she lowered her hand to his private parts until she felt the flinch of his body rejecting her.

"If you don't want me, beg me to stop," she said, pulling herself on top of him, straddling him while his headless mistress watched. Emile's chest heaved up and down. He squeezed his eyes shut. His breath smelled heavily of licorice from the anisette. Zahlah pressed her breasts against him, waiting for his body to relax, for his arms to reach up and take her. Emile remained rigid, keeping his arms down at his sides, his face averted from hers.

"Don't you see how much power you have over me?" she asked.

His eyes would not open to see her face.

"I think you don't love me," she said.

"I do," he whispered. The corner of his eye tensed.

"Then what? You think I'm ugly? You're afraid of me?"

In the silence, his breathing trembled.

"It's true. Isn't it?" She exhaled a hot breath onto his wincing face. "You are the man with all the power, and look at you, you are afraid."

"I'm not afraid!" he said, eyes open now, looking at the wall.

"Oh no! Of course not," she taunted.

His face reddened with anger. "I love you," he said.

She pulled her torso up to look at him sternly, to see him cower beneath her. "No. You only love me in the quiet control of clothes," she said.

Zahlah quit the bed and saw her dark reflection in the full-length mirror, her body hard and ugly, her nipples righteously erect. An American woman. That's what she saw. Liberated and humiliated. She grabbed a dirty robe from the hamper and left the room to sleep by the empty pool.

5

The next morning Emile would not speak to Zahlah, wouldn't even look at her over the top of his *Los Angeles Times*. She walked from room to room, ignored, invisible to him, until he went out to the patio to finish reading his paper. By noon, she noticed that he'd vanished, leaving his newspaper on the lounge chair.

It was almost 2:00 p.m. when she heard Emile calling her name from the patio door, talking enthusiastically in English as he entered.

"There you are," Emile said in Arabic. The bald journalist appeared behind him, holding up his black camera and his sack for lemons.

What was this? Zahlah wondered. An invasion in her own living room? The two strolling in like grinning allies, the journalist waggling the camera at her.

"This man wants to see my clothing designs," Emile said. He explained in Arabic that he'd been talking to the journalist for an hour now, that the journalist knew fashion designers and boutique owners who could help him, people who wanted to see original work. "Go put on the wool coat," Emile told her, his voice full of authority. Zahlah waited for an enigmatic smile to relieve her from the room, but there was only the wave of his hand.

In the bedroom, she unboxed the ancestral coat. It seemed too precious to wear in public, too personal to be gazed upon by strangers. Her *sitta* was right there in the bottom button. Zahlah emerged from the bedroom, cradling the lapels close to her body, no longer warmed by the affection sewn into the sleeves or the loving squeeze of each stitch.

The journalist snapped two photos, then said, "No . . . no." He shook his bald head as he approached her. Without hesitating he reached up to her throat where she'd fastened the top button. He lingered there, and she thought that he'd come to liberate her, that their eyes would lock, and he'd pull her toward him to kiss her, right in front of Emile, placing his warm tongue into her mouth the way Americans kiss. Zahlah's lips parted, wanting the kiss, wanting it for herself alone, to ease her longing for love. No kiss came. He didn't even look into her eyes. Instead he placed his dirty thumb on her ancestor's face, smearing his fingerprint over the glass. His crabbed fingers went down to the next button, and the next, until the coat flapped open against her dress. Backing away from her, he shooed her out of the room with his voice.

The journalist spoke only to Emile now. They negotiated in English until Emile finally told her to put on the silk gown.

Zahlah, opening her mouth to protest, was stopped by Emile's hand, his finger pointing like a knife. "It is finished," he said. "Put it on."

She retreated, outraged, her mouth soured by her own silence. In the bedroom, she stripped the despicable dress from the dummy and put it on, transforming into Emile's American mistress. The sleeveless bodice fit snugly. What had seemed so glamorous now looked fragile, about to rip at the seams, barely able to contain the body of a real woman. That's what she'd become. In Beirut she'd been a girl, but in America she'd gained weight and grown hips and breasts that filled out the dress. No longer the paper doll he'd married. No longer so easy to silence. And yet here she was, her head full of noise, and she could say nothing, not a sentence in English.

"So this is America," she thought, full of contempt, as if America couldn't get any worse, but in a few weeks she'd discover things *had* gotten worse. Her mother and *sitta* would disembark a boat cheering, "America! America!" Zahlah would be told that everyone was so happy until they realized they'd been deceived, arriving in Senegal, not America, swapping their homeland for a third-world country, and there was no legal recourse, no return ticket home, not even a safe home to return to. Civil war would break out, and bombs would explode in Beirut, destroying the seaside resorts.

When she came out from the bedroom, the journalist clapped his hands once, then said something to Emile, some word of praise for the gown. Emile responded by demonstrating the artistry of the skirt, the surgical precision of the line. He drew out the flounce of the gown and held it straight and proud, then let it drop in a lush wave that sent the skirt into a creamy swirl above Zahlah's feet.

The journalist snapped a picture of Zahlah standing alone. He stepped back, inspecting her. Not quite satisfied, he smoothed a hand along her waist, preening the gown. He acknowledged only the dress, not her, taking one picture after another. Finally, he posed Emile and Zahlah side by side, together but not touching. Zahlah could not smile. Shutting her mouth, she stared out at the camera to conceal the stone in her throat.

"Like a wedding portrait," Emile said quietly, in Arabic, before the camera's shutter released. "The only thing missing is the veil."

When it was all over, the journalist held out his empty sack to Zahlah, showing her the twiggy stems at the bottom of the bag, instructing her to go outside. "Lemons. Lemons," he said, the only English she understood.

PIRATES

"Ever think you're going to disappear someday?" Kilroy asked. She drummed the steering wheel with her index fingers. "Know what I mean? Like you could fall down a rabbit hole and vanish from the face of the earth?"

Mike didn't respond. He angled one of the air conditioner vents onto his face. Kilroy was making him nervous, making him feel stupid for hopping into her car.

"I used to think like that, like I'd disappear someday," she continued. "But now I'm starting to wonder if I might drive down a street in Salt Lake City or Madison, Wisconsin, and see a girl who looks exactly like me, driving the exact same car, but traveling in the opposite direction. Don't you ever think about that, Mike?"

"I have no idea what you're talking about," he replied. "You don't have any gum, do you?" Mike popped open the glove compartment and found a pile of Triple A maps, but no gum. He rummaged through the crumpled hamburger wrappers and ATM stubs crammed around the handle of the emergency brake.

"Hey! It's not nice to go through other people's stuff." She leaned across him to shut the glove compartment.

Mike was seventeen. He didn't know this woman whose car he'd hopped into. The only thing he knew was her name—Kilroy.

Earlier that day, Mike had been standing on the curb outside Blue Beard's Fish and Chips trying to attract customers when Kilroy pulled up. The classified ad for his job had said, "Hiring Teens for Exciting Promotional Campaign at Fast Food Franchise" but neglected to mention that he would spend five hours a day waving at cars in a pirate costume. All day he'd been standing on the corner in the soupy heat, clowning for Blue Beard's. Now and then a car honked at Mike. People waved. No one stopped. It occurred to Mike that he wanted someone to stop. Anyone. And finally someone had.

Kilroy parked her gold Honda hatchback right in front of Mike and rolled down her window. He walked up to the Honda, squinting to see who it was. Swing music played on her radio. She switched the radio off and said, "Hey." Her lips curled up at the edges. A rumpled map covered her legs.

"You lost?" Mike asked.

She tossed the map onto the back seat. "Sort of," she replied. "I'm looking for Motel 6. Know where it is?"

"Yeah, it's about ten minutes from here."

She looked at her watch. "If I get lost I'm screwed. They'll give my room to someone else if I don't show up before eight."

"I can tell you how to get there."

"Won't work. I have no sense of direction. I get lost all the time. I know this would be a huge favor, but do you think you could get in the car to show me how to get there? I swear I'll bring you right back. I'll buy you dinner or something."

"I don't know," he said and glanced back at the restaurant. He brushed sweat off his forehead with the oversized cuff of his jacket. The girl in the car was twenty-something with long curly hair; he liked the way it looked. Her face was cute, maybe a little too pudgy. "I'd like to help you out, but I don't get off till eight."

"Oh," she said. Her face lost its radiance. "That's okay. Never mind. Can you at least point me in the right direction?"

He pointed east, toward the orange roof of a Waffle House, and as soon as she drove off, he regretted what he'd done. Maybe it had been the kindness in her eyes, a kindness that most girls refused to extend. In high school, the girls who caught Mike's glances shut their faces like doors—all smiles turned off; the flicker in their eyes went out. For the first time in his life, a girl with an open face was asking Mike to come in. All he had to do was say yes. It was that simple—say yes—but he'd been too afraid to say it despite the fact that only thirty minutes of work were left, and he despised the job and the hot costume he was forced to wear. His wallet and credit card were buried in his pocket. If he had wanted to, he could leave his change of clothes behind. It had been stupid to let the opportunity go. Stupid, so stupid. Helping her would have been honorable. Now he could do nothing but insincerely wave at the hot pulse of cars that kicked dust into his eyes.

Funny how his mother always warned his little sister not to get into a car with a strange man, he thought, his sister Michelle with her over-glossed lips and purple eyeliner and short little skirts. Mike's mother never warned him about anything. He could be independent, reckless, even stupid. His mother never said to him, "Don't get into a car with a strange woman!" Michelle was taught to protect herself by saying "No," yelling it loudly: NO! Mike was taught to never hit a woman, to never even touch a girl unless she permitted him to touch her, and so he never did anything at all with a girl. For all of his sister's training, he didn't think she ever used the word "No."

Mike lived with his mother, his sister Michelle, and Grandma Evelyn. His grandmother was his only ally in the house. Before his grandfather asked for a divorce, when

Mike was three or four, Grandma Evelyn would pick him up in her white Cadillac for Sunday babysitting. She didn't dote on him then. Instead she watched him play on her waxy kitchen floor while she smoked Virginia Slims and clipped coupons at the table and told him to "calm down" in a husky voice. Now, in her seventies, she chewed gum and wore polyblend slacks with sleeveless shirts that exposed her freckled shoulders. She told him that he was lucky to be raised by women, that he'd make a good husband some day; he'd be a real fine man who keeps his responsibilities, not like his father or grandfather. Once a week she'd rummage through her purse to fish out a rumpled ten-dollar bill that smelled like Wrigley's Doublemint. "Take this and go buy your girlfriend some chocolates," she'd say with a wink.

At ten minutes to eight, the little gold Honda with the swing music pulled in front of Mike again. The girl rolled down her window, smiled, and said, "Hey."

"You didn't find the motel?" he asked.

"No. So . . . what do you say?" She patted her hand on the passenger seat. Without saying yes or no, he got in and shut the door behind him.

Now Mike fidgeted and wished he had some soda to quench his thirst. They'd been driving and talking for five minutes.

"So where are you heading?" he asked.

"I was thinking of heading back to your ship. You're a pirate, aren't you?"

He looked down at his brass belt buckle, the wide cuffed jacket and baggy black pants. "I guess so. I'm not really sure what I'm supposed to be."

He set the three-cornered hat on his lap and kicked the fast food containers and CD cases that surrounded his sneakers. The sneakers were the only remnant of himself; the rest was a disguise.

"You eat at Taco Bell a lot," he said.

"So?"

"So, you know the meat in their tacos, it comes in these giant bags with all this orange grease staining the inside of the plastic. I worked there for two months."

She shrugged and watched the fender of the truck in front of her. "You aren't what you eat. You're what you do." She lifted her foot off the brake. Her bare legs were sharpened with stubble.

"What do you do?" he asked. "I mean, for a job."

"I left my job. Now I just drive, travel, that kind of thing. You're welcome to come with me for a day. I wouldn't mind driving you back home if it means I have some company."

"Really?"

"Sure."

Kilroy drove to the edge of town where the border frayed into a truck stop with gas stations, chain restaurants, and motels. Beyond the truck stop the land was flat and uncultivated. Kilroy's car rattled over a set of train tracks. Mike gave her the remaining directions, and she pulled into the lot of a Motel 6, parking the car near the lobby.

"Should I stay in the car?" he asked.

Kilroy riffled around the backseat for her purse and pulled out a black tube of ChapStick. "No, come with me." She smoothed the ChapStick over her lips. A sweet, medicinal vapor perfumed the air. "We'll give the clerk something to talk about. He can tell everyone there's a pirate in the motel." She opened the door. Humidity spilled into the car along with the electrical buzz of cicadas.

"Can't I wait here?" he asked before she got out.

She put her hand on his leg. "Are you sure you want to stay here?"

Mike nodded. Warmth from Kilroy's hand pressed through his nylon pirate pants.

"Okay, then, I'll be right back." Kilroy closed the car door and stretched, raising her arms over her head so her tank top hiked up and revealed the pale skin on her back. She walked toward the lobby and straightened her rumpled shorts with a tug before pushing open the glass door. Red lines scored the back of her legs from sitting in the car. Mike looked at himself in the rearview mirror. His face was flushed. With a ketchup-stained napkin from the floor, he soaked up some oily perspiration around his nose. His matted hair, mussed from his pirate hat, was too sweaty to rake with his fingers. He kept an eye on the glass door of the lobby and thought he saw Kilroy turn around to check on him. It was hard to tell. The glass reflected his own image huddled in the Honda.

He wondered what that pat on the leg was all about. It was more like a squeeze but just barely a squeeze. It definitely meant something. He felt paranoid. Out of the corners of his eyes, he thought he saw some passersby wink at him. They knew. They all knew. That was how he felt about Kilroy: she *knew* and she was messing with his head, but he didn't know what she knew. She had some kind of power that made him feel off center.

Kilroy came out of the lobby dangling a key on an orange diamond-shaped key chain. She knocked on the car's window. "So are you coming along or what?" she asked.

The summer had been boring until now—nothing to do, no girls to date. It wasn't just the pink nail polish on the moons of her nails or the auburn tendrils draped over her shoulders that had brought him to this motel; it was a boredom that he had neglected to acknowledge until now. Finally something was happening, and Mike didn't know what to do. He fumbled for the common sense that had escaped him the moment he got into her car.

"Well . . . what are you waiting for?" She put her hands on her hips. The orange diamond swung from her fingers like a lucky charm.

Mike watched the slice of skin between her shorts and shirt. "Where will we go?" he asked.

She crouched down and cupped her hands over the window. "We aren't going anywhere. Don't you get it? The point is just to go." Pale freckles stippled her cheeks and nose. She had a doll's face, like the dolls his little sister used to play with, dolls with round cheeks, bristly eyelashes and spooky marble eyes. "Are you afraid of me?" she asked with a laugh in her voice. "I'm just a bitty woman. You think I'm gonna hurt you?"

"No."

"Okay, then make up your mind."

Kilroy went to the trunk. Mike got out of the car. The air outside stank of manure. A windy moan from the cars and trucks on I-80 hung on the breeze like the call of a raptor soaring over the land. It was the sound of something coming, something circling and closing in on him.

Kilroy slammed down the trunk and walked up the concrete staircase with a duffel bag. Rubbery flip-flops smacked her heels. Mike searched the cars and pedestrians in the parking lot of the Perkin's restaurant across the street. People knew him here. People might see him with Kilroy.

Kilroy took her flip-flops off at the top of the stairs and padded down a line of aqua doors. Mike's footsteps warbled metallically against the stairs and railing. From the second floor, Mike could see through the open foyer to the other side of the motel where two white grain silos sprouted out of the fields like the stalks of enormous decapitated mushrooms. Beyond the silos, where the sun was going down, a necklace of headlights beaded the dim highway. Mike followed Kilroy, passing drawn curtains and air conditioners sucking hot air out of each room. Kilroy stopped at a door over the lobby and unlocked it.

"Always the same," she said after she opened the door and flipped on the light switch.

Cold air slapped Mike's face as he walked in behind her. The room smelled faintly antiseptic.

"It's my seventh day on the road, and I've stopped at Motel 6 every night," she said. "I can never get over the sameness. There's the same quilted bedspread, the same floral wallpaper, the same glass ashtray on the same table." She chopped her hand toward each item. "Only the room numbers change."

Mike sat down on the leaf-patterned bedspread. The mattress creaked beneath him. A nightstand with a television remote bolted onto the wood separated two beds.

"Each morning I wake up and wonder if I'm moving forward or moving in circles back to the same motel each night," she continued. "I'm even starting to think that I'm cloning myself each time I wake up in one of these cloned rooms. Maybe part of me is rising up like a ghost to move on, and the other part is staying behind. Eventually I'm going to turn around, drive back across the country, and catch up with one of my clones."

"You aren't serious about this clone stuff, are you?"

"I'm serious about the sameness," she said. "It's unhealthy."

Kilroy walked to the back of the room and into her reflection in the vanity mirror above the sink. Blue veins trailed the back of her knees. The Kilroy in the mirror was looking at Mike. "You mind if I use the john?" she asked.

"Course not."

As soon as the bathroom door clicked shut, Mike inspected the room. A Bible and telephone book lined the drawer of the nightstand. Under one of the beds, he found a pencil and book of matches with a phone sex ad on the jacket. He pulled back the curtain and peered out. A cadaverous priest with deep hollows in his cheeks opened the door to the neighboring room. The priest looked in Mike's direction before unlocking his door.

"There's a priest in the room next door to us," Mike said when Kilroy came out of the bathroom.

"Is he tall and skinny? Mostly bald?"

"How'd you know?"

"I've been traveling with him for two days. I saw him at the Motel 6 in Omaha last night."

"He might be following you."

"Don't be ridiculous. We're probably moving in the same direction." Kilroy pulled the sheets back from the bed where she'd put down her duffel bag. The pink soles of her feet slid under the covers. She turned on the television and sat with two pillows propped behind her back.

Mike stretched out on the other bed. He watched Kilroy and tried to read her body language. She chewed her cuticle as she watched television. Then she crossed and uncrossed her ankles under the covers. He was waiting for a sign, either a wink or a nod or even a paranoid sign blurred by the vision of the corners of his eyes. She folded her arms beneath her breasts. Her eyes locked onto the television screen, and suddenly she was far away.

Kilroy was almost as far away from him as the two teenaged girls who went to the Rec Center swimming pool that summer, girls he watched from across the blue rippling water. One girl always dipped her toe into the pool but never jumped in. There was something conspicuous and needy about the way she walked to the pool and back to her towel. Her white bikini was too tight, and the skin under her arms bulged around the strap. The other girl swam laps between the splashing kids and dipped beneath the string of blue-and-white buoys marking the deep end, oblivious to everything around her, intent on tagging the wall and turning around. After swimming laps, she rested against the inner ledge of the pool and removed a pair of goggles that left red raccoon rings around her eyes. When she walked by Mike with chlorine-clean skin and drizzling hair, he was too intimidated to say, "Hello." He had never been acknowledged by either of those girls. Even though Kilroy was sitting in the same room, the aisle between the two beds was like a body of water separating them.

"I need to call my mother," Mike said. "Maybe I should go home."

Kilroy brought her quilt-covered knees to her chest. "If you go home, you won't come back."

"But my mother will worry."

Kilroy examined a loose plastic thread from the stitching in the quilt. "Fine. Call her." Her voice sounded bruised.

Mike hesitated, then picked up the phone and read the sticker that contained dialing information. The phone's red button-light cycled on and off. What would he tell his mother? That he wanted to spend the night with a strange woman who had invited him on a road trip? He could already hear the word "No" clanking out of his mother's mouth like a cage door slamming shut. Without calling, he hung up and flopped back down on the bed. Kilroy was changing channels with the remote until she found a movie that was starting.

"I've seen this movie twice this week." She curled up under the covers and shut her eyes.

Kilroy was testing him by feigning sleep, Mike thought, but he didn't know how he was being tested. Either she wanted him to call his mother, or she wanted to see if he would run away. He decided he would wait her out. He would pass her test, whatever the test was.

Mike alternated between watching the movie and watching Kilroy. On the television, cars crashed and police sirens blared. Kilroy didn't stir. Her mouth was open. Her breathing was nasal and heavy. Mike couldn't concentrate on the movie. The undertow of Kilroy's presence distracted him too much, so he slid off the bed and knelt beside the nightstand to examine the greasy crinkles of her eyelids and the pouty peaks of her upper lip. She didn't wear makeup. The light freckles on her nose seemed to form a pattern.

Mike reclined on his bed and noticed a blue cellophane-tipped toothpick harpooned into the cottage cheese ceiling. If he took out the toothpick, he imagined the ceiling might float away and reveal the darkening sky, the first tips of the stars, and his destiny coded into the planets and moon. His life felt determined by celestial navigation.

Mike stood on the bed and pulled the toothpick out. From atop the bed, Kilroy looked small and sweet. It occurred to Mike that she trusted him. She wouldn't have invited him along if she thought he were a pervert or a freak. He swizzled the toothpick between his fingers and looked back up at the ceiling. No sky. No stars. No destiny. Mike was starting to believe that *destiny* was just a fancy word for randomness.

Jumping down from the bed, he reclined on the mattress and thought about home, first imagining his room and then his sister's voice on the other side of his bedroom wall. Fumes from her wet nail polish always seeped into his room. In the kitchen, his mother would be removing her blue real estate jacket and sorting through the mail, not noticing that Mike wasn't home.

The diamond key chain sat on the bed stand. Mike picked it up and quietly left the room. He walked through a veil of warm air. The sun had set. He went down the pinging stairs and looked for a soda machine. When he found it, the priest was there gathering ice into a plastic bucket. The pirate and the priest. Together they looked like two actors who had jumped off a stage, abandoning their roles midperformance. Mike wouldn't have felt so silly if he were really a thief, an explorer, or someone who fit the part. The priest slipped a cube of ice into the pocket of his cheek. Their eyes met when Mike stood under the yellow light where moths flickered. Mike glanced in the direction of a gurgling truck docked at the gas station beside the motel. He expected the priest to preach the virtues of logic and say, "Go home, boy. It's the right thing to do." The priest said no such thing. Instead, he crunched the body of a dead cicada under his shiny black shoe and walked away with his bucket of ice. Mike bought an Orange Crush and a Milky Way. He glanced at the miniature mouthwash, aspirin, and toothbrushes in the toiletry vending machine. His home was only two miles away.

A train-crossing signal clanged when he started up the stairs. The approaching train rumbled and rat-a-tatted on the railroad ties. In the distance, the high red lights of the radio tower winked. Halogen lamps illuminated the semis and dusty cars in the motel parking lot. Hunkered over the trunk of his car, the priest brought out an open box containing pamphlets and set it on the pavement.

When Mike reached the top of the stairs, there was Kilroy, leaning against the railing outside their room.

"Hey," she said, her voice calm and drowsy. "I thought you got scared and ran away." She stretched her arms over her head, yawning, then did a little swivel-and-quiver gypsy dance to the blowing horn of a train. "You can leave any time you want," she said. "You don't have to go anywhere with me."

Mike extended the diamond key chain to her. "Do you want me to leave?"

"No." She folded her fingers over the key chain and brought it to her chest. "I want you to stay."

From the door, Mike looked into the room at the rumpled beds. Kilroy's duffel bag and flip-flops were strewn across the floor. The room seemed more inviting now. Mike stepped inside, into a cool fold of air, and sat on his bed.

"I ordered a pizza," Kilroy said from the doorway. "I thought you might be hungry."

"Good."

She closed the door. "Why don't you take off your shoes? Get comfortable."

Mike pushed his shoes off with his toes. They landed between the two beds. Then he took off the jacket and tossed it to the floor.

"There. Happy?" he asked.

"What are you mad about?"

"I'm not mad about anything. I guess I'm confused," he began, feeling like he was about to tell her everything, to admit that he had never done anything like this and that there were places he wanted to explore that he couldn't get to by car or plane or boat, places within himself that he wanted to reach but couldn't find the way. Or he could find the way, but he needed to navigate dark constellations to get there. These places were the untapped depths of himself: sensual places, dirty places, spontaneous places, assertive places. If only he could break open his flesh, he might find a whole treasure of pomegranate rubies inside himself, each ruby an undiscovered place. He felt that he was on the verge of discovering one of these places, but his brain paused on the moment of discovery, and the star-mapped skies closed shut.

"What is it?" she asked.

"I want to know more about you," he finally said. "What were you like in high school?"

"Oh, let's see. I was into a lot of kooky things." She smiled and brought up her feet to sit cross-legged. "I read tarot cards and palms, and I stared at the ceiling and tried to project my astral body out of my physical body. I tried to move objects with my mind. I was never quite in this world, if you know what I mean. I was always floating somewhere above it."

"Were you trying to escape?"

"I guess, but I wanted out of reality, I mean *way* out of reality, into another dimension."

Mike leaned over the aisle between the beds and offered her his hand. "Will you read my palm?"

Kilroy uncurled his fingers and traced her nail over the creases of his palm. Nerve endings awakened in his hand.

"What does it say?" he asked.

"I don't know. Isn't that sad? I've forgotten everything. I only know the names of the lines. Head. Heart. Life. Fate."

She folded his fingers as though closing a gift box she'd opened and pushed his hand toward his chest, giving the gift back. Had he stopped her from giving his hand back, had he put his palm on her face, then perhaps he would have left the imprint of his fate line on her cheek. When she left, she would take his fate with her. Or was it his head that he was so afraid of losing? Or his heart? He'd never realized how much of himself there was to lose. Or how easy it would be. Or how good it would feel to sink his fingers into her nest of curly hair and give up every scrap of himself.

Mike looked down at his ragged cuticles.

"So what are you confused about?" she asked.

"I just wondered where we're heading."

"We're just going to go. Pick any road. Doesn't matter which one. Wait a minute. I think I hear pizza coming." She got up to peek out the curtains. "Yep, it's coming."

After the pizza guy left, they sat on their separate beds, watching television and eating.

"We'll be leaving early," Kilroy said after they'd finished the pizza. "You'll need your sleep."

She reached over the nightstand and turned off the television with the remote. Mike switched off the overhead light and slid under the clammy bedsheets. Someone shuffled down the corridor outside the room. Kilroy rolled in bed, sniffled, and plumped her pillow, then settled again. Mike shut his eyes and tried to forget that Kilroy was sleeping in the bed beside him. He thought about the swimmer and how the musculature on the swimmer's back was developing into smooth lines and angles. She was becoming strong. He'd seen the change in just six weeks. He wanted to tell the swimmer how much he admired her perseverance, how much he admired her newfound strength. All of her hard work was sculpting her body into something wonderful. He wanted to tell her all this without sounding like a fool who was infatuated with her. In truth, it wasn't her body that he marveled at but her transformation. She had shed her old skin and become something new.

At dawn, Mike awoke to rustling paper. Kilroy was reading the map of the United States. A slit of light shined through an opening in the curtains. Kilroy straightened the map with the palms of her hands, leaning in close to survey the jagged face of America. She scrutinized the wrinkles and creases in the paper. Her finger delicately touched the red and black lines cutting through the states.

Mike sat up on his elbows.

"We need to check out." She refolded the map. "Then we're going to breakfast. My treat."

Mike got out of bed and went to the bathroom. His chin was fuzzed like a camel hair jacket. He was starting to look more like a pirate. He splashed water on his face and dried it with a starchy towel. When he came out of the bathroom, Kilroy opened the room door. A pamphlet, lodged into the crack of the door, fell to the ground.

"What is it?" Mike asked as he put on his shoes.

She tossed the pamphlet on his bed. The cover said, "God is the Way." Mike weighed the pamphlet in his hand and was about to open it, but he didn't want to look inside. He crumpled the pamphlet up, then tossed it in the trash.

The humidity had settled into a comfortable morning mist. At the bottom of the stairs, Kilroy handed Mike her car keys and duffel bag.

"Can you put this in the trunk?" she asked.

He went to the parking lot. The priest's car was gone. Mike popped open the trunk of Kilroy's car, put the duffel bag in first, then placed his pirate hat over some heavy rope and bottles of motor oil. Kilroy came out of the lobby when he slammed down the trunk.

They got in the car and took 380 south to 394. About now, his mother was probably crying over her lost son. Phone calls were being made. He felt terrible about what he was doing to his mother. It just had to be done. Already Mike felt different, more alert, more himself. They drove down the narrow two-lane highway, passing miles of farmland.

Before long they were in Missouri and passed through a red tollbooth where an old lady held out her cupped hand for the twenty-five-cent toll. Some tourists had stopped their car to take a photo of the tollbooth, snapping pictures to remember the trip after going back home.

Kilroy eyed the tourists in her rearview mirror. "Yep," she said. "I bet my clones are out there sending postcards to my apartment as if a part of me is still there, stuck in that stagnant life. They're sending postcards that say, 'Greetings from the Grand Canyon' and 'Greetings from Milwaukee.' On the back of the postcards, they're scribbling, 'Wish you were here.'"

"I doubt it," Mike said.

"You know what else? I'm taking a minor across state lines. That means I'm officially a criminal." She nodded her head. "I always wanted to be an outlaw."

They drove through Wayland Junction onto Highway 61. Fireworks stands appeared every few miles. Mike felt the grooves of the road beneath the tires. Highway 61 cut through a few small towns with unpaved crossroads. They occasionally paused at a stoplight or stop sign where the entire town was just a bar, a cafe, some gas stations and a post office. After they drove through each small town, rows of corn reappeared.

Over an hour passed before they approached the city of Hannibal. An institutional high school stood to their left. The highway sloped down to motels and restaurants.

"Look," Kilroy said, pointing to a person a block away.

There was a kid on the curb in a pirate costume outside Blue Beard's Fish and Chips. He was doing a foolish dance as he flagged cars off the highway. Desperate for attention, he jumped and waved and shouted at cars like a man who was drowning or dying, like his very life depended on just one car stopping. In a backward glance, Mike watched the image of the pirate shrink into the distance.

"Wave good-bye to yourself," Kilroy said. "Wave good-bye."

THE MAN FROM ISTANBUL

Every other night that summer they ran the length of Route B. Michael, half a block ahead of Elle, bobbed up and down. No cars at 10:00 p.m. No people. Just Michael and Elle and the amazing flat greenness of Iowa.

They lived in Swisher, a place stopped in time, unaffected by recessions or economic booms. The main street had one bar and one gas station with old-fashioned yellow-and-blue pumps that said Sunoco on their faces. Three flagpoles stood in a grassy median with American flags that chimed their ropes against the poles. A few homes sprouted from the edges of town, and the blacktop receded into gravel roads and low fields of soy, except for Route B, which ran the two-mile length between Swisher and Shuyville, a dead-eye run, with no streetlights, only fields on both sides of the road.

At the opposite end of Route B, in Shuyville, stood another bar and another gas station with old-fashioned pumps. Like running into a mirror, Elle thought.

On their run home from Shuyville that evening, Michael turned to look at Elle behind him. The air smelled wet. Frogs from an unseen pond chirped. Michael jogged backward to talk to Elle.

"I used to think that frogs were the voices of the dead," Michael said, panting softly. "I read it in a children's book when I was a kid. They were the dead calling out to the living, to their lost loves."

Elle and Michael had met at a reading at Prairie Lights Bookstore. His thick dark hair was textured with wax, and his glasses were out of style. He was awkward yet attractive in a scholarly sort of way. She mistook him for a thirty-something grad student, like herself, not a professor. They talked about the intersections between postmodern rhetoric and film theory, a conversation that seemed a million miles away from frogs and lost loves.

Michael turned to run backward and lifted the hem of his shirt to wipe off his face, revealing a pale, dewy stomach. "You okay?" he asked when he put his shirt down.

"Yeah." Elle barely caught enough breath to respond. "I'm okay." She was reminded of a story about frogs that she wanted to tell, one of dozens of stories that she hadn't told him yet, but she was too out of breath to talk.

Michael got a second wind and sped up, running ahead of her. His foot patter grew more distant. Sweat burned into Elle's eyes, and she trundled onward, far behind Michael. Her pulse beat into her eardrums all the way home.

By the time she reached the wooden porch of their house, Michael was inside stretching against the armrest of the sofa. Elle opened the screen door, huffing and sweating. Michael watched her as he curled a leg behind himself and stood like a flamingo. He yanked the toe of his shoe to stretch his front thigh muscle.

The frog story was still on her mind, her own frog story. Elle picked up a glass of water that she'd left on the coffee table and guzzled it down. "My ex-husband once told me," she began breathlessly, "about a horror movie he was working on when he first got out of film school. It was a horror movie about frogs."

Michael grabbed his other foot and stretched. She took the last swig of her water.

"He had to film the money shot where all the frogs are just sitting, hundreds of glistening frogs just sitting and staring at the camera. When it came time to shoot the scene, they filled this room full of frogs, but the frogs wouldn't stop jumping all over the place."

She bent over, panting. Michael waited for her to finish. "So anyway," she began, "they nailed each and every frog to the floor."

Elle remained bent over. The harder she breathed, the more she seemed to sweat. Michael stopped stretching. Without responding, he walked into the kitchen and turned on the faucet.

"What is it this time?" Her voice followed him into the kitchen.

"Nothing," he replied. He came out with a glass of water in his hand.

"C'mon. What is it?"

"Your stories," he said.

"I'm sorry. It's a terrible story. What kind of person would nail a living creature to the floor? I'd forgotten all about it until you mentioned the frogs."

The muscles in his thigh twitched. "I'm going to bed." His voice sounded reedy, shrinking away from her as he walked up the stairs.

She sat on the sofa and wanted him to return. When he didn't, she went up to their bedroom door. It was shut. She was sure she heard him in the bedroom talking on the phone. His voice sounded like an agitated stage whisper. She left him to himself and went to the bathroom to wash her face and brush her teeth.

Michael had a way of being unpredictably sensitive that made Elle feel as if she'd been cruel to him, more like a teenager than a thirty-three year-old woman. Even after six months of living together, he had no patience with the awkward nuances of their relationship, with the fumbles and miscommunications. It didn't take much for him to cubby himself in his office to research his book. Lately he'd been worked up about whether he'd make tenure after a colleague's disastrous tenure review.

Elle entered their bedroom a few minutes later. Michael was reading in bed with a copy of Plato's *Gorgias* on his lap.

"So who was that?" she asked.

"Who was what?"

"On the phone. Weren't you talking to someone?"

"I was reading out loud."

His running shoes were flung at the foot of the bed with the laces still tied in a knot. A thin white cotton sheet covered his legs and waist. Underneath he was naked, and she wanted him to ask her to get naked too, but instead he sat there with his book perched on his thighs. He didn't watch her slide off her running shorts. When she took off her shirt, she used it to dry herself, still sweaty from the run, hair tousled and damp and curly. Michael didn't even look up to see her remove her jogbra.

A fan overhead moved stale air in a circle. Elle stood there, bare-chested. Yellow light from the bed lamp spilled over Michael's book. He kept his head down, the dull thud of Greek in his ears.

When they finally moved in together, it was because Elle had been so damn tired of being *between*—between her apartment and Michael's house, between careers, between cities. Her divorce from Heinz had been final a few years earlier, and now she was practically engaged to Michael. She hated how her whole life seemed broken and without continuity. Her past was cut into clumsy polyhedrons, each corresponding to a different relationship in a different house, a different job, a different car. When she met Michael, she just wanted wholeness again.

Elle and Michael lived in a two-story wood-shingled house with a creaky wooden porch swing where they could sit and watch fireflies on the lawn or farmers putter up from the fields in rusty Ford trucks. She had given up her Iowa City apartment in a five-story brick building near Prairie Lights Bookstore for a life of solitude while she worked on her PhD dissertation, a collection of academic essays on film noir. Meanwhile Michael composed a book on the intersections between postmodern and classical rhetoric. He wrote in an upstairs room full of sunlight that revealed how lusterless and dry the floorboards were. Beyond his window lay a field of young tender soy, endless rows of green, with only the occasional truck rucking up a cloud of dust in a narrow field row. Elle's office looked onto Route B, where she could see cattle being driven to slaughter during the day and at night could watch the mosquito fogger truck spray a cloud of pesticides into the air.

Within the confines of the continental United States, this home in Swisher seemed like the farthest point from her childhood home in the Hollywood Hills. Her family's property line trailed down a steep hillside that bordered the back lot of Universal Studios, where trams of fatted tourists drove through ridiculous landslides and flash floods. A favorite studio-tour trick was to cruise down the main street of a Wild West town, then drive the tourists behind the storefronts and saloons to show they were only facades, just the faces of buildings propped up on wooden stakes. It struck Elle that the whole purpose behind the Universal Studios Tour was to show people how they'd been deceived.

Elle liked Iowa for being exactly what it was—not phony or pretentious or false. As much as she liked the isolation of Michael's house, she sometimes worried that the house had no history, no ghosts, no tattered edges of Michael's former life with his ex-wife Leah. During the long summer days, when the rooms upstairs became too humid for writing, she walked by Michael's door and momentarily listened to his clatter of typing. While he was locked up in his mental activities, Elle was free to wander the two stories of the house, opening closets and looking through drawers. In the basement, where there could have been some tangible remains of Leah, Elle found nothing but boxes of paperwork from his years of teaching and stacks of final exams in bluebooks unclaimed by students. On the first floor, the storage cabinets in the pantry were devoid of clutter. Upstairs, in their bedroom, he lined his shoes neatly over the floorboards of the closet. She once walked through the dusty drapery of clothes to a hidden spot where boxes could be stored, secrets kept, and still there was nothing. It occurred to Elle that she wanted to find something. Anything. A scrap of nostalgia. A longing for permanence. Instead, she felt like they were living in this house temporarily, keeping all of their personal baggage packed, only inhabiting their relationship until the lease was up.

The next evening, Elle stood behind Michael and watched the image of him in the mirror. He'd grown a dark scruff of facial hair since classes got out in May and was looking more bedraggled than scholarly. They were freshening up for a rhetoric department party, so Michael decided to shave. Coarse black hair stuck to the sides of the sink. Elle noticed the brown mole on his cheek, big as a pencil eraser. She'd forgotten it was there. The more he shaved, the more he looked like a stranger to her.

"Last night I dreamt of a secret room in this house," she said to Michael, "and I found boxes of things that you'd been hiding from me."

In the mirror, his mouth tensed; the line of his jaw grew more defined. "I'm not hiding anything from you," he said.

"I didn't say you were. It was just a dream."

He dragged his razor down his cheek. "What's this dream supposed to mean?" he asked, then brought the razor to his other cheek.

"It's just the dream of the secret room. I've had it in every house I've ever lived in. I thought everyone did."

"Well, I haven't." He rinsed his razor under running water, then looked at her in the mirror where she leaned against the pink bathroom tiles. "So what did you find in the boxes in the secret room?"

"I can't remember." She lied. "I think the boxes were full of books."

"That's all?" His face was so close to the mirror that she couldn't see it; she could only see his hand holding the razor against the side of his jaw.

In truth, when Elle opened the largest cardboard box, she found his ex-wife Leah's corpse curled into a fetal position with her hair limp and sticking to her face. A dark joy had filled Elle's soul. Here was the corpse that Michael couldn't get rid of. When Elle knelt closer to inspect the body, she discovered that it wasn't a corpse at all, but a scarecrow woman with long elephant grass for hair and a body of twigs and twine. The white frock that the scarecrow wore was Elle's, not Leah's.

That evening they went to a party held in a grassy backyard under low Chinese lanterns. Rhetoric grad students mingled with professors. Elle tried to blend in but felt as if Michael's colleagues were comparing her to Leah. It was a silent comparison, a nod of the head, a feeling of being appraised. Carl, one of the more personable professors in the rhetoric department, had insinuated that he didn't like Leah when Elle met him earlier that year. It was clear in the way he smiled at Elle, in the paternal way he praised her and patted her on the back. Elle had to piece these things together, the tiny nudges and smiles.

She'd been looking for Carl and finally found him alone in the kitchen washing dishes. Elle sidled up to him and put her hands deep into the suds, nudging him aside so she could wash while he dried. She chatted him up by talking about her dissertation on unstable ontologies in film noir, about the way film noir destabilizes the known universe, turning it into something no longer easily understood. "Even people can become unstable ontologies," she said.

"Like our parents," Carl replied. "People no longer easily understood. Christ, my own father had photos of another woman in his desk drawer when he died."

"Your father was an antihero," she said. "Mine was just an accountant."

Carl laughed a deep laugh. He had the presence of an aging stage actor still capable of self-deprecation—the smooth baritone voice, and the dark, dignified features. "He had audio tapes too," Carl said. "Those old reel-to-reel tapes from the '50s. He had her voice on those tapes. Just talking. Mostly she talked about how she wanted to know everything about him. And her voice, it was so . . . I don't even know how to describe it . . . eerie and disconnected from her body, like someone in a trance. I could only listen to those tapes a few minutes before feeling disturbed. But even after stopping the tape, I'd return an hour later or a day later to hear more."

"You must have been mortified."

"I was in my fifties, too old to be mortified. I'd already been divorced twice, made my own mistakes. Different mistakes. Not cheating. Nothing like that."

Elle pulled her hand out of the suds and took a sip from a wineglass she'd brought into the kitchen.

"I'm sorry," Carl said. "I'd been mulling it over recently. Sometimes I'm still stuck in that old place. It was twenty years ago that I discovered those tapes and my father's secret disgrace. And here I am, still discovering those tapes, still trapped in that emotional loop." Carl dried a glass and carefully placed it on a cabinet shelf. "I don't understand deceit. I know that sounds naïve, but it's true. I couldn't lie to my family like that."

Elle nodded and looked down to scrub a dish under the soapy water. Some guests had migrated into the living room, where Dr. Klein was telling a story. She could hear people laughing. Outside salsa music was playing. Elle held her hands under the water and felt a spoon, then a knife. "What were your mistakes? If you don't mind my asking."

Carl lifted his head to think, his eyes moist and blood-shot. "My mistake was toeing the pool instead of diving in," he said. "I wasn't 'all in' in my first two marriages. I held parts of myself back." He picked up a plate and dried it off in a circular motion. "I didn't trust my wives. I either trust someone or I don't."

"Michael mentioned that you didn't trust Leah," Elle said, though she was lying.

"Did I say I didn't *trust* her? I might have hinted to him one time or another that I didn't care for her much, but I never said anything outright."

"Maybe it was obvious."

"*She* probably said something. Michael wouldn't have picked up on it."

Elle handed him a wet dish, and Carl took it absently, still sorting out his thoughts. "Michael was always so damn in awe of her," he said. "But Leah could be abrasive, overly opinionated. And she was always reading between the lines. Nothing got past her." He finished drying his dish and placed it on the shelf. "You're much nicer." He smiled, try-ing to pass it off as a compliment.

It was insulting, really, to be compared to Leah. Leah and Michael had been college sweethearts, both virgins when they met. It seemed absurd to be compared to a woman who'd had one lover and then gone straight from college to graduate school, a life of sexual and academic se-clusion. Meanwhile, Elle had been out there living, really living—making films, navigating a rocky marriage, simultaneously succeeding and failing in the real world. And people had the nerve to call Elle *nice*?

In Hollywood, *nice* was an epithet, a career killer. During a brief period during college Elle worked as an actress. She'd already done a few small movie roles and got in touch with a brittle sixty-year-old agent who wore heavy makeup and reeked of cigarettes. After five minutes of interviewing Elle, the agent said, "Listen, honey. I've heard enough. I'm just not seeing a real person here." Elle was only nineteen, still a girl—not yet divorced, not yet bitter or judgmental, not crafty enough to realize she was supposed to sit in front of an agent and put on a show by exaggerating her personality. Up to that point in her life, Elle had been too cautious to be a real person. Not being a real person, that's what Elle now feared the most—being nobody all over again. It was okay to be nobody at the age of nineteen. But at thirty-three, experience had turned her into somebody. Not a fake somebody, but a real person with a real past. With the agent, Elle had thought it a good quality to *not* be a real person. "I can become anything you want," was Elle's reply. But the agent said, "You've got to be someone right now. You've got to *be* somebody all the time. You can't just turn it on and off. Look," the agent finally said, "I'm not seeing an actress in front of me. But you seem like a very nice girl."

A nice girl. For some reason, that was the part that stung.

"Listen," Elle said and turned off the running water to get Carl's attention. "I'm not so nice." It came out weak, lacking conviction.

Carl laughed out loud, a hearty laugh that traveled into the other room. "Of course you're nice!" he said. "You're the nicest person I know."

Elle and Michael left the party early that night. It was only 10:30, so they watched *The Lady from Shanghai*. Halfway through the movie, Michael went into his office to write, and when he didn't come to bed with her, she sat on their mattress and worked on her dissertation. She was still jotting down ideas on the last scene in *The Lady from Shanghai* when Orson Welles tries to shoot Rita Hayworth in the hall of mirrors, a laughable scene by today's standards. Welles can't see Hayworth because he sees too many of her. No singular Hayworth exists.

Elle had been writing on Hayworth when Michael walked into the bedroom already wearing his running shoes.

"Let's go for a run," he said.

"It's already past midnight."

"I've been writing for an hour," he said. "I need to clear my head. Come on."

That evening, when Elle and Michael were running between Swisher and Shuyville, Michael started talking about anarchy and pataphysics in postmodern rhetoric. Topics she knew nothing about. Elle dodged dark plugs of manure in the road and tried to keep up, but Michael kept getting ahead of her.

"Slow down," Elle finally said into the darkness. "Tell me a story."

Michael turned around and ran backward for a moment. "I've run out of stories to tell."

"Then make something up."

He was silent for a while, then turned, jogging onward. Elle ran in the darkness behind him, running toward the silvery glint of reflectors on his shoes. She waited, and eventually he said, "If we run fast enough, if we run hard enough, we can run straight from here to Istanbul." He paused. Cricket song filled the space between them.

"Imagine it," he said. "We can run straight through to an evening street bazaar where vendors are folding their wooden tables and rattling olive-shaped worry beads on long tasseled strings. You can smell the spicy incense." He slowed to run alongside her. "Beyond the street bazaar, I point to a red door, and we enter a motel. Behind the reception desk, a door leading to the domestic dwelling of the motel caretaker exudes the smell of allspice and food simmering over low blue flames. A half-awake child with enormous dark eyes stands in the dwelling's doorway. 'We need a room,' I say to the boy, and from under the reception desk he produces a key, not a flat key, but an old-fashioned round key that fits in the type of keyholes that children can peep through."

Michael broke from the story. Elle could hear him breathing. They were running into darkness, between open fields with not even a light from Shuyville visible ahead of them.

"Go on," she said.

Michael was quiet for a moment, his feet landing gently on the road. "The boy leads us up a flight of stairs. At the end of a hall, he points to the door that will be our room. Then he motions to an open door beside our room where the bathroom is," he continued, "I enter the room, but you go into the bathroom. There's no shower, just a stained tub. The bathroom has a yellow-tinted mirror and an iron-stained toilet. When you look into the mirror, you don't see yourself. Instead the mirror looks straight through to the room where I am. I'm on the bed, naked, waiting for you on stale linen sheets. After you bathe, you come to me but realize that I'm not me anymore. I'm a familiar stranger, someone you've merely passed on a street dozens of times but never officially met. When we look into each other's eyes, we are both unsure, just strangers, you see, until I smile, sheets over my torso, chest bare and damp with sweat from the run."

In Shuyville, they turned and ran back. When they reached their home, the house was dark and the windows had been left open, so the warm moist heat from the outside was now inside.

"Don't turn on the lights," Michael said.

She followed him upstairs to the bedroom, to their low bed on the floor without a bed frame or headboard, just a box spring and a mattress, and Michael sat on the edge, drew her toward him, and took off her running clothes. He placed his hands on her wet skin, then ran his fingers up the perspiration on her spine.

That night she fell in love with the man behind the mirror; it was the other Michael from Istanbul that she was loving as he recited the rhythmic opening from *The Iliad* in ancient Greek, the drumbeat of poetry pulsing through her body, chanting about mortals who cut deals with gods.

In the morning Michael was Michael again—Michael who had run out of stories to tell, Michael who read Aristotle out loud in Greek as he waited for his coffee to brew, Michael who shut his office door to work all morning and afternoon.

"Don't interrupt me today," he said. "Don't even knock on my door."

Meanwhile she went down to the basement and scavenged through several boxes she'd never unpacked—old sheets, impractical high-heeled shoes, items from her home in Brentwood. Then she opened one of Michael's boxes by accident and peered inside at the childhood items she'd unearthed—a tiny plastic human skull, a leather sack full of dominoes, an unopened pack of BlackJack gum. She was hoping to find something bigger, beyond easy comprehension, a personal history he'd been hiding from her, the other lovers, the life he'd been running away from like Robert Mitchum in *Out of the Past*.

With her ex-husband Heinz there were twenty-five years of clues to his former lives. Heinz was fifty when they met. Elle was a twenty-five-year-old director's assistant working on his film crew and doing bit parts in his films. A whole graveyard of dead relationships littered Heinz's past, so many that he couldn't remember all of the names. With

Michael, there was just Leah. His One. A whole number. Elle was merely his Two. Second place. A mere understudy number. Not quite good enough for the starring role.

Forty-five. That was the number of men Elle had dated in her life. She'd counted them one day and was embarrassed that the number was so high. Granted, twenty of them were in high school and junior high, just boys she went to the movies with once or twice, nothing fancy or sentimental. She only had sex with the guys she was serious about, so she'd only had sex with eleven. Not terribly adventurous, she thought. Yet it would forever be held in contrast to Michael's One.

The next evening, Michael went to the university's main library in Iowa City to research his book, leaving Elle alone. After he left, Elle turned on some *bosa nova* music and opened a bottle of wine. She remembered a stash of cigarettes in her desk drawer, a relic from another life in L.A. when she smoked and drank and went to parties once a week, a life Michael barely knew about. She never mentioned the movies she'd acted in. Michael had a tendency to cringe when she brought up Hollywood, especially in front of professors.

Elle had to hold her hair back to light her cigarette on the electric stove. The tip didn't catch at first, and surprisingly, when it did, it didn't taste as bad as she'd expected. In fact, it tasted exactly like the first time she'd ever smoked, kind of exciting, like she was getting away with something by smoking in this kitchen with its white porcelain sink and daisy wallpaper.

Michael was supposed to be in Iowa City for a few hours. She could take a bath in the clawfoot tub upstairs and air the smoke out of the kitchen. Before she had a chance to finish her cigarette, she heard Michael's Honda pull onto the gravel in the driveway. He'd only been gone ten minutes, and the next thing she knew he was walking up the wooden stairs of the back porch and coming in through the kitchen door, catching her smoking. It was twilight outside. His arrival brought in a stray june bug that plinked against the ceiling light. Michael dumped his book bag on the warped floorboards and looked at her.

"Look who's back." Elle took a drag from her cigarette. "Did you forget something?"

The june bug continued to plink against the light. Elle ashed her cigarette into the sink, then took a sip of sour red wine. She was still feeling pretty good, too good to act defensive about the random cigarette she was smoking or the bottle of wine she was drinking by herself.

"Fine. Don't say anything." She stared back at him—a challenge—waiting for him to make some curt remark.

Instead he took the cigarette from her hand, gently, and she thought he was going to douse it with water under the faucet. He then took the pack of cigarettes, removed one for himself, and lit his own cigarette off of hers before handing it back to her. Together they looked at each other, blowing big gusts up to the light where the june bug was thwacking itself. They were in some kind of standoff. He wasn't talking. She wasn't talking. Eventually he grabbed the bottle of wine she'd opened and took a swig, being deliberately rough about how he tilted his head back, then wiping his mouth with the back of his hand when wine dribbled down his chin.

"Follow me," Michael said. He flicked his cigarette in the sink and began taking off his clothes.

Upstairs he stood in their bedroom naked for a moment, stared at her, then kicked around some dirty clothes on the floor. Under a pair of jeans, he found his running shorts and put them on, so she changed into hers.

Again they went for the evening run. Michael took the lead down Route B, into the dusk. Still not talking, she followed. Her lungs were tight with smoke.

"Tell me another story," Elle said.

"I can't."

"Please."

Elle was keeping a good running rhythm alongside him. It wasn't too dark yet, so they could run without worrying about what their feet might land on.

"It's going to be harder this time. You'll have to run faster." He sped up a little and moved ahead of her. "If you run fast enough and hard enough, you'll be able to run through walls."

Elle was running to keep up with him now. "Slow down," she said.

"If you want a story, you'll have to run faster," he said. "Imagine that we're in our house, and you can walk into the walls, between the fusty joists and beams, sliding sideways into creaky corridors where the electrical wiring runs through the house like a network of blood vessels. I can hear you sometimes. I hear you standing in the walls, breathing, watching me from between the cracks. Sometimes you watch me work at my desk. You scuttle about like a cockroach, moving from one room to the next. I've heard you under the floorboards, too. I've even placed my foot down where you were trying to lift a board to peer at me and held my foot there, keeping you down."

"What am I searching for?"

"What *are* you searching for? That's precisely what I'd like to know. I hear you scratching around all the time, especially when I'm working, so one day I run fast and hard, and I follow you into the walls, chasing you through the maze of corridors, not just trying to corner you but to reach inside of you, to run straight through the wall of your skin and hear your thoughts. And so I catch you by my room, in a space behind the closet, and I run at you hard and fast, and we run right through each other—just like that—and I see you run out from behind me, back through the wall and into the house, so I peer between two boards and see you in my office. There you are, and you are me, inside my body, and I am in yours. And I watch you sitting at my desk, working, and it is *me* working. Me. That's it. That's all I see."

The next morning, in the yellow light of dawn, when a lone farmer walked the field rows picking weeds, Michael became the man from Istanbul again. With sweaty bedsheets twisted around his legs, he pulled Elle toward him. His body language was relaxed. He didn't talk, and as long as he remained silent, he could be anybody.

In the following days, sometimes Michael would smile mischievously or stroke her shoulders instead of speaking, and it was as if he'd slipped into the man from Istanbul. Eventually he stopped shaving, and an ethnic-looking five o'clock shadow grew in. He looked almost Arabic—dark eyes, dark facial hair. The hair on his head was overgrown and getting curly. Pomade wouldn't hold it down anymore, so it fell over his eyes. His skin was tan from summer gardening. But the minute he started talking about rhetoric, his personality reverted to plain Michael again, the uptight professor, the man locked behind his office door.

As the weeks passed, the movement between those personas became fluid, unexpected; all he had to do was reach around her waist while Elle washed dishes, and she knew which man she was dealing with. It was as if his cerebral persona was gradually being replaced by a sensual one. With his old cerebral self, everything was clinical and safe. This new persona was volatile and exciting. The transformation finally seemed complete when Elle caught him in the backyard dancing. He'd been gardening and had brought out a radio to listen to NPR, but the news had changed to Lebanese music with cymbals and sweeping violins and a singer chanting *habibi habibi habibi*. When Elle heard the music, she walked into his office and looked out the window. He was standing there with his hand up to his eyes, staring at the radio, and must have felt Elle looking down. He smiled up at her and drew his arms out, snapping his fingers, swiveling his hips. There he was, the Man from Istanbul, opening his arms and inviting her to join him.

Soon afterward, their habits changed. Michael stopped obsessing over his book, stopped staying in all night. Instead he and Elle went to bars or parties with grad students. It was Michael who suggested that they run to Shuyville, get two shots of Yeager at the Crowbar, then run back to Swisher where they could get another shot at Joe's Bar if they felt like it.

Michael started out playful on the run to Shuyville that night. His skin tone had grown dark, and his chest muscles were toned. He ran bare-chested and kept a spare shirt rolled in his back pocket.

"Tell me a story," he insisted on Route B, in the darkest part of the run.

Running felt good to Elle. It was the end of the summer, and she no longer got winded. "I'm no good at stories," she replied.

"Tell me anything, Elle. Anything." His voice had become intense, putting pressure on her to perform.

"All my stories are too long," she said.

"Then tell a long one."

Elle felt like the girl in the agent's office all over again. She didn't know the right story to tell. Things were going so well with Michael that she didn't want to spoil it with a story. She'd worked hard to become something, somebody, a person who wasn't nice. But with Michael she suddenly wanted to be a blank, a void to be filled, a screen upon which he could project any identity.

She thought about her dissertation instead. It would be much easier to go back to that place where they met, where they talked about ideas instead of themselves. She wanted to talk about fragmentation in film noir, how noir breaks the illusion of unity.

"Never mind," Michael said. "Forget it. You're thinking too much." Michael ran silently ahead of her, his mood completely soured. Elle said nothing, not a word. No stories. No theories. No talk of ideas.

When they arrived at the Crowbar in Shuyville, Michael stopped running and put on his shirt. He was being deliberately silent, not even looking her way when Elle paused to catch a breath by a streetlamp swarming with moths and gnats.

"Give me a minute," she said, but he'd already entered the bar. A satellite dish sat in the lot with pickup trucks parked on gravel. *For Sale* flyers for tractors and combines papered the entrance.

Inside a few men wearing seed caps turned to look at Elle.

"You could have waited for me," she said as she sat beside Michael at the bar.

Michael shrugged and said he'd already ordered two shots.

The Crowbar was almost identical to Joe's Bar in Swisher, except this bar had a map of the United States where a bar mirror should be. Elle longed for their reflection—the two of them joined side by side. The map said "You are here" on top. Where there should have been one star marking Shuyville, Iowa, numerous gold schoolteacher's stars dotted the map.

Elle rested her arm on the surface of the oak counter. The place stank of stale cigarettes. Two men glanced at Elle over the tops of their beers. Her hair was tousled and stringy from running, her white T-shirt damp with sweat.

Elle turned to say, "I thought they'd have a pool table," but Michael didn't reply. His white shirt was clinging to his skin. He took the crew neck and drew it up to wipe off his face.

Michael stared at the TV above the bar and sucked in his cheeks. A '70s horror film was playing, a film Elle didn't recognize—a young woman in a skimpy slip was fleeing a man in a white theater mask.

"I saw you in a movie once," Michael finally said without looking at Elle. "Just after we started dating. You were being murdered."

Elle was taken by surprise, almost afraid to look up at the TV to see what was happening on the screen, afraid she might see herself up there. Michael kept staring at the movie.

"I told you I'd done bit parts," Elle said. "Nothing worth bragging about."

"No. It was nothing worth bragging about." His voice darkened. Michael's jawline went rigid as he stared at the TV. It was humiliating to watch, seeing that woman run for her life.

"Make someone turn that TV off," Elle said. A shiver of perspiration ran down her back. She wanted to invoke feminist film theory. The male gaze. The lack of female agency. The objectification. Like the woman on the screen, Elle had merely been the object of that gaze. But there was more to it than that. The only horror film she'd made was directed by her ex-husband Heinz. Her relationship with Heinz had been on the rocks and ended the night of the film's wrap party. The producers had rented the Castaways Restaurant in the hills above Burbank, clearing out one of the dining rooms so people could dance. By the time Elle and Heinz arrived, everyone was already drunk. While Heinz went out to the dance floor, Elle sat at the bar and watched actors and crew members. She watched as though they were all far away from her. The thrill of seeing actors had died. It was just a party with a lot of drunk people whom she didn't really know, although she seemed to know them since she'd seen so many of them in movies, but there they were, exposed, themselves—not pretty, but plain; not handsome, just dull.

Heinz was dancing with the actress Sharon Knight. Sharon was drunk, enjoying the dance, swinging her hips into Heinz's groin. It was not jealousy that Elle felt but tedium. Everybody was only acting happy, pretending to have a good time, forcing themselves to make the most of the bad horror film Heinz had directed.

While Elle watched Heinz dance, a German man at the bar turned to her and asked if she was an actress in the film.

"I think my character is called Dead Girl #2," Elle replied, then explained that Heinz needed to shoot an extra scene, that he needed an actress to say things like 'Help me' and 'Please God, no!' before being cut into pieces. "He buries my hands in a corn field," Elle said. "My feet end up in a garbage bag. I don't know what happens to the rest of me."

The German was an older man, conservative, in a pearl-gray suit. "You shouldn't see the film. It will be very disturbing for you to see yourself being cut into pieces," he replied.

"It won't be me," Elle said. "I'll see that girl as someone else."

He shook his head. "It will be you," he said. "You will hear your own voice screaming for help."

At that moment Heinz came running back to Elle, hurt, literally hurt, with a handkerchief held to his ear.

"Sharon Knight bit my earlobe," he said. "Look." He held out the white handkerchief to show Elle the blood. "She damn near bit through it."

Behind him, Sharon Knight tiptoed toward them, giddy, hand over her mouth, acting twenty years younger than she was. "How rude of me!" she said.

Sharon Knight inspected Heinz's ear, too drunk to be clinical. When Heinz looked down at the bloody handkerchief, it was no longer Elle's husband that she was watching but his doppelganger. The actress was not *the* Sharon Knight but a sloppy stand-in, her double—the Sharon Knight who gets hit by cars and tossed off cliffs. The real Sharon Knight wasn't something that could be contained within her skin. Even the actress Sharon Knight was merely an idea created with soft lights and the right setting, a persona that existed only in the context of heightened surroundings. Outside of that context, she was nobody, seeming to be nothing but skin without a *self* inside. That's what Elle was seeing: Sharon Knight's skin.

Elle was about to tell Michael this—about Sharon Knight's skin—when Michael put his fist over his mouth and exhaled loudly through his nose.

"It was just a bad film," Elle said. "What are you so upset about?"

Michael shook his head, seeming almost disgusted. "It was you." And just like that, Michael winced in a way that let her know the long spell he'd been under was broken: Michael was Michael again, not the Man from Istanbul but the Michael who sequestered himself in his room, the Michael who overreacted unexpectedly.

Elle looked up at the map, wanting to go home instead of sitting in this bar where everything felt wrong, as if they'd run too far, and now they were in some other place where neither one of them belonged, as if they'd broken through the looking glass and tumbled out on the other side.

Michael knocked back his shot, then pushed himself from the bar. "You know the sickest part of all," he said. "The camera doesn't look away like a decent person would. It kept looking as the ax cut off your hands one at a time. Like you were just a prop. And the ax was the actor."

"It wasn't me," Elle said. "Just the close-ups were my face. Jesus, you're making too much of this."

Elle didn't know what else to say. All she could think of was Sharon Knight's skin, how skin was merely artifice, an illusion of self and nothing more. This is what she wanted to explain when Michael stood up and threw a handful of dollar bills on the bar.

"Don't leave me here," she said. "It wasn't me. I was just acting, just playing a role." Michael was already walking away. Elle looked up at the map on the wall, looked for Istanbul, but instead saw all of the stars, dozens of schoolteacher's stars stuck on towns and cities all over the map—stuck in Ohio, stuck in Idaho, stuck in Iowa.

BILL SUGGS' SAFE HOUSE

The last time anyone saw Fitzpatrick was the summer when cats overran the Safe House. The old farm cat, weeks after birthing a litter of eight, stalked the perimeter of the house, teats hanging heavily from her chest, as she searched for her mewling brood under the porch or behind the hen house. This was ten years earlier, when the Safe House was still in use, before state agencies opened shelters in Columbia and Booneville. Women would sneak kittens into their rooms when Bill Suggs wasn't looking, tiny weights cradled in their hand-me-down skirts. Back then, some tom still lurked in the tallgrass of the woods, slinking up to the back porch, waiting for the mother cat to coyly curl her body around the rail post. The cats gave the long summer days a lurid sexuality contrasted only by the queer innocence of grown women sneaking kittens into their bedrooms at night.

At present, the Safe House was empty except for Bill and a few offspring of those cats. The house stood far from town on a chert backroad that edged the countryside and river bottoms, a place where the mail was delivered by a fellow in a blue pickup truck. His name was Howard, that man in the blue truck, and the women who once lived in the house knew everything about him—who his wife was, what church he attended, where Howard went to high school— yet he knew nothing about the women except that all the mail arrived under Bill Suggs' name and the women wore the same box-stitched shawl from one to the next, and whenever a new woman came, another one left, but the shawl . . . it stayed behind.

These were women who staggered into police stations at four in the morning with nowhere else to go, wives of professors at the university in Columbia, daughters of shop owners, girlfriends of grad students; most were not born in Missouri but became trapped in it, with no family to claim them nor friends to take them in.

The home nearest the Safe House was a trailer on ten acres of land, alone in the middle of a field without a truck or a car or even the tracks of a bike running toward it, just leggy grass and ragweed and goldenrod crowding it in. The man who lived there did not want to be seen, did not pick up the mail delivered to a rusty box at the edge of his land, did not want to be bothered, or so it seemed. That man was Fitzpatrick, and that was all the women of Bill Suggs's Safe House ever knew.

A family portrait of dead women greeted anyone who entered the Safe House. This was the first family, the farm builders, six women in dark 1860 clothes with sharp white scalps showing through the parts in their dark hair. The matriarch stood like a ghost in the middle, her five daughters seated around her, all of them survivors of the crazed guerrilla warfare that ensued years after the Civil War ended, the years of fighting and murder in Missouri. The men who once lived there were long dead, killed by Unionists, leaving behind women with faces weary from death and forearms muscled from farm labor. In those days it fell to the women to clean the corpses, and Bill Suggs imagined this photo was taken not long after these women had cleaned the murdered bodies of their men, their naked mortality given one last embrace by tender female hands. You could see it in each woman's eyes, that each one had clasped hands white with death, that the wife had held her husband's cold fingers while her daughters sponged blood from his brow.

When Bill Suggs bought this house in 1972, she bought it from Eleanor Suggs, an eighty-year-old woman born illegitimate on the same oak table where men had been cleaned before burial. Eleanor wanted nothing of the house, nothing of its past, and left the old portrait of women and the treadle sewing machine in the front room and the long oak table for Bill Suggs.

Bill Suggs was only thirty-one when she took on the Suggs family name, the name of the father beaten to death by guerrillas in 1866. Her old name was a ghost to her, her old self. She took the name Bill Suggs because she needed to vanish, and the name was generic and comfortable and pleasantly masculine, masculine enough for her to wear trousers and old flannel shirts.

Bill started the Safe House when there were no women's shelters in Columbia, when she herself—a young graduate student in psychology—had to pack up her things and run. Instead of running to the home of a friend, or running to colleagues in the department, she spent the last bit of her inheritance on this two-story farmhouse ten miles outside town, so far into the country that no man, she thought, could reach her.

This man, Fitzpatrick, her nearest neighbor, was a man with a reputation of self-imposed isolation. In all these years, only one person—a middle-aged woman—had wandered into Pierpont Market looking for him. No one got her name before she drove onto the gravel road toward his trailer. The owner of Pierpont said she was pretty and well-dressed, that she wasn't wearing the kind of shoes for high-footing it through weeds and wasn't driving the kind of car that could make it through the elephant grass leading up to his trailer.

No one had seen Fitzpatrick for years. Now he'd suddenly resurfaced. Bill first encountered him by the creek filling plastic milk containers with water. The creek, a ten-minute walk from her house, opened into a slow-moving pool which she called the River Bill. She liked to go down to the River Bill at dawn to take a leisurely swim that made her feel completely in her skin, thrilling at the chill of water. It was the only time she let her hair down from its long braid, letting it unravel into S's along her spine.

The morning she saw Fitzpatrick, the sun was not yet warm, and she'd just removed all of her clothes, taking everything off to dive down into the cold water, diving down to the bottom until her ears popped. As she rose up again to breathe, she swam to a waist-deep area and stood. It was then she heard the twig break. Swiveling around, breasts under her crossed arms, she was staring at a man on the shore.

Fitzpatrick! A sighting more rare than a mountain lion. He wore a long gray beard and raggedy clothes. His eyes widened, opening up for her in childlike wonderment. He'd come from the rough side of the valley where deer found shelter at night, a thicket of fallen oaks and trees with poison ivy climbing their torsos. She'd never been on his side of the creek, though it was easy enough to wade the shallow waters and cross over. Something had always told her it was a line not to be crossed. Now they both stood on the border—his side, her side—and Fitzpatrick stared back in silence, eyes locked, not looking away.

Tiny fish darted downstream, around Bill's legs. A woodpecker in one of the trees tapped out Morse code. Bill hooked her toes around a pebble at the bottom of the creek. Her skin pricked with cold electricity as she braced her forearms against her breasts. She couldn't look away from the man on the shore and imagined that this was the same conflicted fascination felt by two members of warring Indian tribes who happened upon each across a stream—one part entranced, the other part prepared to kill.

And how would Fiztpatrick try to kill her, she wondered. Would he press her head down to the smooth cold stones at the creek bottom until silty water filled her lungs? Or would he slit her with a knife and leave her bleeding in the River Bill? Someone had, in fact, tried to kill her once, because he loved her so very much. She thought a man as old as Fitzpatrick, a man in his mid-sixties, wasn't capable of that kind of love. She concluded that this man called Fitzpatrick who stood like a question mark along the muddy banks of the River Bill with his head tucked low in submission was capable neither of fighting nor of raising a fist.

"Hulloo!" Bill called out like a warm porch greeting to a neighbor passing by.

"H'low," Fitzpatrick replied, voice graveled from disuse.

"I'm naked," Bill said, feeling suddenly stupid for having said it. "Well, I suppose you noticed that."

Fitzpatrick squinted at her, as if he hadn't noticed, then lowered his empty milk jugs to the water and let them fill. Bill waited, watching him, until he finally rose up, looking at her standing there. He raised his hand as if he were confused about how to say good-bye, then loped back into the woods from where he'd come.

The following week, Bill caught Fitzpatrick stealing fresh-laid eggs out from under her chickens. Thinking he was a fox, Bill went to the kitchen door with her shotgun and a flashlight, and through the door's window watched him trundle away, arms cradling half a dozen eggs, the hunched question mark of his body punctuating the darkness. Bill threw open the door and yelled out to him, saying, "Hey, Fitzpatrick! You want some bacon with those eggs?"

Then one afternoon Fitzpatrick came walking up through the fields and came knocking on the Safe House door. Bill had been out picking blackberries and found the old man cupping his hands to the windowpane to peer inside. He waited on the porch, his boot heels thick with mud, his pant legs ticked with tiny seeds and burrs. The farm cat made figure eights around his legs.

"I have nothing," he said when Bill came walking up, then he uncurled his fingers, and held out a tiny rodent skull with its long yellowed incisors still intact. He held it out as though it were some kind of country currency.

Bill took the skull from his hand and placed it gently in her breast pocket. "That'll do," she said.

Bill believed in country justice—in settling all deals with a handshake and letting a needy neighbor steal an egg— so she let Fitzpatrick into her house under the pretext that you save a man who's asking for salvation. His dark smell of sweat and virility saturated the foyer where only women had stood for thirty years. Bill could taste his rank odor in her mouth—the oily taste of hormones—and gulped it down, mouthful after mouthful, filling her lungs.

"You need to get cleaned up, and I won't take *No* for an answer," Bill said as she led him to the ground floor bathroom, where a clawfoot tub sat in the center. Bill drew the bath water with a good foam of bubbles. The old mother cat with her pink teats exposed sat in the doorway, watching the spectacle of the old man, his body hunched on the toilet, his brown slacks ragged at the bottom with frayed threads hanging down.

"All right, mister, we've got to get you undressed," Bill said. "Don't be shy, now. It's not like I haven't seen it before."

Bill stood with a hand on her hip and turned around, waiting until the clothes came off and Fitzpatrick stepped into the bathtub, naked and thin, ribs protruding. He sat there with his knees drawn up to his chest, the bald knee-caps peeking out from the murky water.

Bill held her hands under the water, leaning close to his back, feeling her breath quiver in her lungs as she reached down low with the washcloth and stroked it over his lower back, the smell of him so strong that she had to breathe through her mouth.

"We need to bring you back to civilization," she said. "Bring you back to life." She felt as if she were saying it to herself.

Bill drew out his arm and let it hang over the wooden floor, dripping as she pulled the washcloth out to his finger-tips, gently working the cloth between the webbing of his fingers, then down to his fingernails where she worked the dirt free. She scrubbed away the grease on his palms and wrists, then leaned in close, toward his chest, and brought the cloth under his arms. Every now and then she'd catch herself scrubbing too hard and let out a laugh, not knowing what the old man was feeling with his eyes shut. Finally Bill drew her rag up to his face to wipe away his tears.

This man who had nothing—neither family, nor friends—had come here to learn how to live again, *with* mankind, not *without* it. Bill had to teach him how, just as she taught the girls in the Safe House how *not* to live with mankind, how to say "No" with force, how to distrust strangers, how to always be on guard. Bill had lived her whole life saying "No." And now she had to teach this man how to invite strangers into his home and trust people again.

"We need to begin a few lessons," Bill said, "starting now." Fitpatrick's eyes were shut and his beard dripped water into the tub.

"Say 'Yes.'" Bill told Fitzpatrick. "Keep your eyes closed and say 'Yes.'"

"Yes," he replied.

"Now say it with your eyes open. Looking at me."

He leaned forward, as if to touch her. "Yes."

"Now say it with your mouth but not speaking." His face bent into a craggy brown-toothed smile.

"Now say it with your eyes." He squinted, looking confused. "Now say yes with everything: eyes, mouth, lips."

And he replied, "Yes with everything. Eyes. Mouth. Lips."

There are only so many golden moments in a person's life, moments where all the right colors and images come into focus. It ashamed Bill to think that this was one of those moments, that a man could conjure such a feeling of warmth inside her. In her own mind, she was saying "No." No, she wouldn't let go. Until it occurred to her that the word "No" was the only currency Bill had in this world, and you couldn't buy a damn thing with it.

She finished by rinsing Fitzpatrick's body and hair, ladling a tin bucket of bathwater over his shoulders, then she left him to his own devices in the bathtub. Bill returned only once, with clean clothes—some trousers and one of her shirts—and a toothbrush with paste. She left these items neatly stacked on the toilet seat, and gently told him that he need not speak when he looked up with watery eyes, opening his mouth to thank her.

"It's easy to love a man who's so powerless," one of the girls once told Bill; the girl was speaking of a man who'd beaten her every day of her life. It occurred to Bill that she'd never met a powerless man until now. She felt a screw in her soul turn loose, something that had been turned tight for years, and a new emotion was leaking out. It embarrassed her the way being a woman meant you were always leaking—either tears or blood or milk—all of it seemed like a slow drain on a woman's strength. Bill had stopped crying years ago. Menopause had come and gone. Now this, she was experiencing some kind of emotional seepage. No, it wasn't love, but something else, and she'd brought it all upon herself the moment she let Fitzpatrick through the door.

That night, after feeding Fitzpatrick a tuna sandwich and glass of milk, Bill packed him a box of canned food and coffee, then loaded Fitzpatrick into her old truck and drove him down the gravel road and through the weeds to the front of his trailer where Bill's headlights hit the warped aluminum siding and broken screens on the windows. The place looked cold and abandoned. Bill sat with the engine running in front of his house and remembered, years ago, that she had once sat in a young boy's pickup truck after an uneventful date. The boy worked in a milk-bottling plant and wore rubber gloves all day long. Bill, smelling of stale Doublemint gum, had parted her lips for him. And the boy, all hands, touched her face and body with fingertips that smelled of cheese; everything about him reeked of sour milk.

"Well," Bill said, feeling like she was the one who now reeked of sour milk. "I guess this is it." She nodded toward the windshield. "Time to go home." She said it rather coldly. Fitzpatrick squinted at her, eyes locked.

Bill's heart felt strange and intense inside her chest. If Fitzpatrick touched her, she thought she might put a hand to his throat and hold it there.

She swallowed hard and said, "Here," reaching into her pocket, giving him the white rodent skull, papery and fragile.

Fitzpatrick took the skull in his hand and the box of food on his lap and left. He walked to his door, head bent down to his chest, and turned back once, looking at Bill, the question mark of his body asking, begging, pleading.